A TIME OF ANGELS

Patricia Schonstein

BLACK SWAN

A TIME OF ANGELS
A BLACK SWAN BOOK : 0 552 77166 X

Originally published in Great Britain by Bantam Press,
a division of Transworld Publishers

PRINTING HISTORY
Bantam Press edition published 2003
Black Swan edition published 2004

1 3 5 7 9 10 8 6 4 2

Set in 11/14pt Melior by
Kestrel Data, Exeter, Devon.

Black Swan Books are published by Transworld Publishers,
61–63 Uxbridge Road, London W5 5SA,
a division of The Random House Group Ltd,
in Australia by Random House Australia (Pty) Ltd,
20 Alfred Street, Milsons Point, Sydney, NSW 2061, Australia,
in New Zealand by Random House New Zealand Ltd,
18 Poland Road, Glenfield, Auckland 10, New Zealand
and in South Africa by Random House (Pty) Ltd,
Endulini, 5a Jubilee Road, Parktown 2193, South Africa.

Printed and bound in Great Britain by
Cox & Wyman Ltd, Reading, Berkshire.

Papers used by Transworld Publishers are natural, recyclable
products made from wood grown in sustainable forests.
The manufacturing processes conform to the environmental
regulations of the country of origin.

For the Master: JMC
For the Nobleman: BRL
For my travelling companions: D, G & R

ACKNOWLEDGEMENTS

I am grateful to Romeo Biccari, Ruth Bloch, Geraldine Bennun and the late Anthony Clarke for sharing with me certain memories and experiences which I made use of in my novel.

These are the experiences as a prisoner of war at Zonderwater of Romeo's father, Umberto; Ruth's memory of her father checking the list of Holocaust survivors' names, posted outside Salisbury synagogue, as it was updated; Geraldine's description of her elderly neighbour's drawers full of embroidered linen – his mother's trousseau – unused and perished by time; and Anthony's experience as an Allied gunner officer in Sansepolcro, Italy, during World War II when he did not fire on the building that housed Piero della Francesca's fresco *The Resurrection*, though German soldiers were thought to be in the town.

I also thank my agent, Stephanie Cabot, and my publisher Francesca Liversidge for their enthusiasm in my work and for the fun we had in London.

How is the face of God?
Is that God weeping, over there
on the bench in the park,
all alone,
his back bent, his head down?
Why does he weep?
Is it because life is tearing
along its seams and across its grain?
Has he come down from his place
to look at what we do to Creation?
Has he come to witness
the unravelling of his work?

Figure on a Park Bench, 2002

A TIME OF ANGELS

When Primo Verona's wife, Beatrice, left him for Pasquale Benvenuto, their close friend who ran the delicatessen on the corner of Long and Bloem Streets, Primo cast a spell on Pasquale's shoes so that ever afterwards their laces would spring undone as he walked out of his front door. It was an easy enough spell to sidestep. Pasquale, unaware that it was magic he was dealing with, merely cursed the quality of modern laces and thereafter wore shoes that did not need them.

Primo also prepared two spells designed to harm Pasquale's reputation as the best baker and salami maker in Cape Town. One of these would bring sourness to his renowned salami, his *salame Fiorentino* in particular. The other was to impart the bitterness of aloes to his extraordinary fruited bread and so undermine his culinary confidence.

However, Primo did not activate the two damaging spells; he merely composed them and put them on hold. He withheld them because he was not a malicious magician and had no real wish to harm Pasquale Benvenuto. He wanted only to remind him, often, that Beatrice was a married woman and that she did not belong in another man's bed. This message Primo hoped the shoelaces would convey.

Creating the spells gave him a certain satisfaction, but the truth was, they did nothing to relieve the feelings of betrayal that he harboured in his heart, for he and Pasquale had been good friends for many years. He could not live without Beatrice and slid into a depression.

Pasquale Benvenuto made such delicious meals that he had driven many competing chefs to hang up their aprons and break wooden spoons in despair. (The suicide of the Montebello's *sous-chef*, Riaan Kotze, was attributed to the acrimonious and protracted legal battle fought between him and Pasquale over the origination and proprietorship of the recipe for *polenta alla Madiba*.)

For Pasquale, the preparation of food was not unlike the creation of a fresco or a painting. His kitchen was his canvas; his pigments were the reds, greens and golds of tomatoes, *peperoni*, fresh meats, herbs, eggs and cheeses. So accomplished were his culinary compositions, so utterly delicious – to the eye and to the palate – were his baroque combinations of ingredients, that even atheists, when eating at his tables, might be driven to believe that a God did indeed exist – a God of the kitchen – and that his name was Pasquale. One might have a sense too, at Pasquale's restaurant, that minor gods and benign spirits attended him, for even a bowl of fruit well past its best (pomegranates, black grapes and figs), when served with slices of mild *fontina* or a sweet *provolone*, was enough to convert the most Presbyterian of taste buds.

He worked with great confidence and passion, often calling out to his ingredients, urging them, encouraging them towards the masterpiece they were destined to be a part of. He listened to opera or recited poetry as he worked, delivering from memory Shakespearian sonnets as he carved meats and cut up vegetables. His waiters adored him, loved his volatility, were in awe of his skills, never argued about measures or weights when helping in the kitchen, and never, ever, spoke with any favour of other cooks and eateries while in his presence.

Most other cooks, Pasquale believed, worked in only one dimension. They threw ingredients together, without thought of perspective, simply to arrive at a plateful that merely satisfied hunger. Cooks who were artists of the culinary – and he considered himself master of them all – took into account the essentials of depth and balance with every meal prepared. Importantly, they chose their ingredients with great care and combined them with respect and not a little homage.

'The English cuisine must be the worst in the

world,' he once told Primo when they were discussing the merits of Mediterranean cuisine. 'Followed shortly by the Russian and then the German. Their offerings are a mere confusion of ingredients.'

They were picnicking in Van Riebeeck Park, the two of them and Beatrice. Pasquale had spread a square of bleached calico over one of the cement tables near the river and laid out a feast of breads (*focaccia*, *filone* and *schiacciatina*), sun-dried tomatoes, roasted brinjals and courgettes, marinated peppers, olive and potato pie, mozzarella and *pecorino*, wines and mineral water.

'Just look at the English roast and Yorkshire pudding as an example of gustatory paucity – and don't raise your eyebrows at my words – or the English sponge cake, for that matter. It's dry, spiritless food – completely lacking in delicacy. English sponge can never be compared to such as *panforte Senese* with its moist content of fruits and spices. Or *bostrengo*, a rice cake full of fruits with rum and coffee and cocoa and honey. Actually, now that we're talking about it, I think I'll bake one when we get back. We'll eat it at midnight tonight. With espresso. And *Anisetta*.'

He took a mouthful of wine, and continued: 'A tomato served without garlic, without *basilico* or parsley has potential, yes. I can't deny that, because it's a glorious vegetable. But, we must ask ourselves, does it have character on its own? Yes, indeed, if organically grown and picked when sun-ripened.

And can it be rendered tasteless? Certainly – by the many cooks in this city who are guilty, daily, of destroying the very spirit of the poor tomato and then giving its pulped carcass a deceptive Italian name. If there were kitchen justice they would hang for such a crime.

'Meat not fragranced with rosemary and origanum, not studded with garlic, not marinated in wine, has no character either – it has no *innerness*. You might as well dry your meat on a campfire. Or roast a cat. Actually, that Devonshire in Constantia serves cat, I'm sure of it. People think they're eating hare. And they pay for it. God! The world is full of fools.'

'Let me be the devil's advocate,' interrupted Primo. 'Have you ever tried lamb cooked slowly in its own juices, with no herbs at all, no wine, not even salt and pepper, only onion and carrot, served on plain boiled white rice, or with plain boiled potatoes? There's something to be said for the simplicity of such a meal.'

'Simplicity! Don't be ridiculous!' exclaimed Pasquale. 'You're talking there about food for slaves, for prisoners, for foot soldiers. Not for anyone with taste or discretion. We are both of Roman descent, I remind you of that, Primo. Our cultural make-up is Roman, therefore noble, therefore we eat as *I* cook. Not the way Saxons and Goths cook. Now, here, try this. Taste this mozzarella with olive oil and fresh tarragon, and revise your opinion of simplicity.'

An onlooker would have noted that the party of three picnickers laughed a lot under the wide expanse of the Cape sky; that they touched each other frequently; that the woman with long loose hair that gleamed in the sunlight was exceedingly beautiful; that she had taken off her shoes and was paddling in the shallow waters of the river while the men had their animated discussion. It would have been clear that this was a friendship strong and good. It would also have been obvious, from the way each man glanced occasionally at the woman, as she moved through the rippling of light and shadow created by the overhanging milkwoods and wild olives, that both cared deeply for her.

Although such dishes as his *lasagna verde*, *ossobuco*, *polenta pasticciata* and *vitello alla Genovese* were legendary and without rival, Pasquale's fame rested on the salami he cured and his fragrant fruited breads. 'My father's legacy' was how he referred to the breads. 'Some fathers leave behind money and property. My father gave me the recipe for fruited bread. I could wish for nothing more. But he did give me more, as you see. He gave me my art form. He taught me to cure salami and to cook unspeakably delicious food. I learnt from him how to turn the mere beating of eggs and sugar into sonnets, and the whipping of cream, lightly flavoured with vanilla, into ballads. Mind you, my looks too are his. So I have a lot to be grateful for.'

Pasquale had no time for people who counted calories, who fussed about what was fattening, and who thought creams and butters were unhealthy. Guilt, he maintained, belonged only to the religious – it had no place at the table, and certainly not over the meals he cooked. Food, as far as he was concerned, was to be eaten for the pleasure of it. Servings should be generous and, however much one ate, one ought never to deny oneself the gratification of dessert. A little sweetness and then a bitter coffee were the way to round off a good meal.

His delicatessen and bar, Da Pasquale, stood last in line of a row of Victorian shops that had been restored but never modernized and so retained their architectural charm. It was a favourite meeting place of the local community, a nexus of social energy, open every day from ten in the morning until ten at night and, more often than not, always full. Pasquale's waiters, Lovemore and Dambudzo, were assisted by several student casuals in serving coffees, cakes, meals and drinks to patrons with seemingly insatiable appetites. At weekends the violinist, Lazar, played from a repertoire of Spanish, gypsy, Italian and Greek compositions. He sent music spiralling among the drinking and dining patrons; fusing with the clink of goblets; mellowing the clatter of cutlery and crockery; harmonizing with laughter and chatter; never intruding but always touching hearts lightly so that people felt good being where they were, and lingered long after their meal was done.

Every Saturday night, at ten, Long Street's prominent merchants and proprietors took over the window table to play poker. They dressed for the occasion in black suits, with black waistcoats and black satin ties held down by diamond-studded pins, playing into the early hours – Da Pasquale stayed open until the last hand. The only woman among them, Romana of Romana Florist, also wore black – ritually the same antique full-length velvet dress with ivory silk collar and cuffs.

Pasquale never gambled, though he enjoyed the tension of the often fast and ruthless hands. Primo and Beatrice, when they were all still friends, would also share the evening, as did Dr Adam Baldinger, the local general practitioner – a tall, dark-haired, stately gentleman, never seen without his long black trench coat. These three did not gamble either. Beatrice worked at the bar while Primo, Pasquale and the doctor, debating and discussing philosophical and theological matters, drank espresso – Pasquale's laced with *Strega*.

The questions that recurred most frequently concerned good and evil and the nature of God: Why did evil exist? Was it an external force, an intrusive influence? Was there indeed a Devil at work, upsetting God's plan of perfection? Or was the human soul intrinsically evil? Was God really all-powerful? Or was the notion of the Divine merely an existential legend, a legend seeded and nurtured by religious leaders in pursuit of their own omnipotence?

These questions and their answers struck each other like swords clashing, sending sparks of iron to iron flying about, resolving little but exploring the deep cavities of philosophical and theological debate nonetheless.

'Evil exists, yes!' Pasquale would shout. 'It's called *slap* chips and steak. And Hell exists too, at the Holiday Tavern buffet!'

'Perhaps evil is an external energy,' Dr Baldinger would offer. 'An energy which enters the human psyche at certain times of collective stress, like times of war and conflict. Or could evil be seen to be our infidelities? Our betrayals? Our dishonesties? These negatives which cause harm to others on a greater or lesser scale?'

'Evil is surely just our inhumanity – man to man, man to beast – issues with which God seems not to be bothered,' Primo would suggest. 'It was once believed that sin was the causal agent of disease and calamity and that, in the absence of verifiable wrongdoing, witchcraft and devilry were at play. People called upon God for miracles and redemption. Yet God seemed often, and still seems in modern times, to be absent. Or at least distracted.'

'About the existence of God, I'm not so sure,' Pasquale would argue. 'No religion has adequately interpreted, for me at any rate, the force of God. If I accepted that there is a God, I would still doubt that he is omnipotent, omnipresent, all-pervading, as religions would have us believe. How do we answer for war and mass destruction, if God is all-powerful? Would a caring God not intervene to prevent such horrors?'

'But perhaps God is not caring!' Dr Baldinger would exclaim. 'Why should God care? Why should a Divine force be bothered with the human condition? You know, there is a Yiddish saying – God is not kind. God is not your uncle. God is storm and fire aplenty!'

'God is not your uncle! I like that. Beatrice! Please, the doctor needs a whisky for his wisdom. Primo, more water? When are you going to learn that water is for fields and fishes? At least take a drop of wine with it. Beatrice! Pour me a Cointreau, please. And we need something to eat. Where are all my waiters? Dambudzo! That spinach tart – is there any left? What happened to those stuffed anchovies? Lovemore? Have you gone home already?'

Thus the magician, the doctor and the master cook challenged one another, often furiously, while alongside them the poker hands of Long Street's businessmen flashed as players cursed, shouted or exclaimed with satisfaction.

* * *

here is good magic and there is bad. ... a born visionary and soothsayer, worked in good. With his well-honed supernatural skills he could correct imbalances between negative and positive energies and predict the future (though he never read his own or that of his family). He restored positive vibrations to rooms and houses where conflict or death had left residual negativity. People came from far and wide to have their future clarified and to ask his advice. The police regularly called on him to trace missing children.

His readings of the future were clear and accurate, though he took it upon himself to edit them, toning down bad news and never delivering foreknowledge of death. He did not charge for his services, believing that to put a price on his clairvoyance would reduce its energy. Instead he accepted donations. He kept a bronze urn at the entrance of his consulting room into which his clients dropped generous wads of notes, so he was never short of money. Some also brought him carefully chosen gifts: trays of halva and baklava; portions of *tiramisu*; bowls of chopped herring; slices of honey cake and fruited breads. All bought from Da Pasquale.

Primo's first experience of premonition happened before birth, when, in his mother's womb, he had a vision of her untimely death. His mother's midwife reported that he was born crying inconsolably, clinging to his umbilical cord. She had to wrench open his little fists, so tight was their grasp.

23

'It was a sign, a sign. He knew,' the midwife announced knowingly at his mother's funeral, while other mothers whispered among themselves and tut-tutted with pity. For his mother, wheeling him in his pram when he was but three months old, had misjudged the speed of an oncoming delivery motorcycle as she crossed Wale Street and was struck down. Primo escaped death because she took the impact while the baby carriage shot across the road and came to rest against the pavement. He suffered no harm.

Primo was brought up with much love by his devoted watchmaker father, Eugenio Verona, who was also a collector of clocks and watches, and by his widowed aunt, Lidia. Both were aware of his unique talent and encouraged him towards magic and the supernatural, never letting him doubt his unusual abilities.

His widowed aunt more than filled the role of mother, smothering him with love, care and visionary storytelling. Each night she sat at his bedside and told him wondrous tales of knights and path-finders, of light-bearers, kings and queens and humble folk who championed good and justice. She told her stories with such clarity and magical wonder that the boy could all but see her characters before him on the candlewick bedspread, in the soft glow of his bedside lamp. His aunt's compelling voice opened the volumes of humankind's eternal lore and he would fight to stay awake for fear of

losing one word or one chapter of her fantastic
tales. But, alas, slumber always overtook him and he
would tumble into dreams that had a texture not
unlike the stories she told.

While his widowed aunt enriched his imagination
with the fantastic, his father introduced him to
the discoveries and ideas of Galileo, Copernicus,
Socrates and other luminaries. 'These are among the
true men, the golden men,' his father told him.
'These are the ones whose example we must follow
in this transitory life. Not the warmongers, not
the mad men who rule the world, but these, the
philosophers, the astronomers, the poets, the artists,
the explorers – those who hold life in awe, who
question, who postulate.'

Eugenio Verona taught his son Hebrew and Latin,
not sending him to school until he was eleven,
but educating the boy at home. Primo learnt about
time and precision and the exact and extraordinary
workings of the universe. His father also explained
that time and space were infinite and so, early on,
Primo came to understand his mortal size in relation
to the depth of the cosmos.

On nights when the sky was clear, father and
son would look out through their telescope at the
universe, marvelling at the great and systematic
placement of stars and movement of planets. 'We are
looking at the history of stars, my little one,' Eugenio
told his young son. 'What we see twinkling from
space is but a story from long, long ago – the story of

stars. No one knows whether the light we see is from stars that still live. They may be dust already. Or cosmic ash. And in their place there may be million upon million of new stars whose light we two will never see, for their light will only reach our planet when we are long dead.'

In the background of Primo's enchanted star- and story-filled childhood could be heard the comforting and ever-present tick-tocking of his father's many clocks. There was something else in the background, though. Something secret, black and horrible, something seldom spoken about, seldom externalized. It had to do with the darkness of the human soul, for both Primo's father and his aunt Lidia were survivors of the Nazi Holocaust and neither had properly come to terms with their macabre experiences of that genocide.

Though by day they led composed and seemingly contented lives, at night, during the deep hours of darkness, they were each confronted by recurring grotesque imagery stamped upon their psyches. They never spoke about the hells that clawed at the edges of their sleep, nor about the keen hatred with which men turn upon one another. These nightmares they kept to themselves, gasping in disbelief as they woke each morning to find that they were indeed still alive.

Yet it was all there, the opposite of the good, counterpointing the fantasies and innocence of childhood. Eugenio and Lidia's experience that evil was a more powerful energy than good, that good was a mere butterfly in the face of a storm, influenced Primo and fuelled his questioning into the nature of these opposing forces and the drama they continually enacted in the arena of the human soul.

Primo's house in Kloof Street (the extension of Long) was the last in that road still used as a home. Here he lived and, until Beatrice left him, practised as a soothsayer. In its time the area had been a residential one of good standing, but now most of the houses had either been demolished to make way for high-rise office blocks or renovated to serve as fashionable restaurants and architectural studios. The pavements teemed with opportunistic homeless people who loitered, begged, drank heavily and fought among themselves. Feral street children roamed around in packs. These two groups gave the area an unpleasant undertone.

This was the house Primo had grown up in. Built in the late 1920s, it was semi-detached and single-storeyed. He occupied both sides, using the front door of number 21 as his professional entrance and 21A as his own. Each side had a passage leading down the length of the house to a large farm-style kitchen, Primo's father having broken through from the kitchen of 21 to that of 21A. There was some duplication: two sinks, two back doors, two built-in *credenze*, two bathrooms leading off the passage and two deep tiled fireplaces.

On one side were the fridge and stove and a large Oregon pine table with four bentwood kitchen chairs. On the other side stood his father's reflector telescope, pointed at the skylight, through which Primo still studied the stars and planets. There was also an ottoman couch, faded and in need of re-upholstering. A large worn Bokhara, its colours softened by time, covered the wooden floor. Primo's father had taken down the wall dividing the two back yards. There a garden of shrubs and herbs grew, with a mature mulberry tree in the centre.

Leading off the passage of 21A were the bedroom, lounge and a permanently locked room. In the lounge stood an art-deco sofa with two matching armchairs and a second worn Bokhara. An art-nouveau lamp, its base the curving figure of a woman, was placed in the corner. A display cabinet protected a collection of small porcelain animals, a bag of marbles, a fairly valuable Susie Cooper tea set and a blue Venetian glass jug. On the wall hung framed reproductions of Dante Gabriel Rossetti's *Beata Beatrix* and Evelyn de Morgan's *Aurora Triumphans*.

The bedroom was simply furnished with an uncurtained and uncanopied four-poster double bed, a wardrobe – still hung with most of Beatrice's clothes – and a dressing table, its drawers untidily stuffed with the underwear she had left behind. The window was curtained in thick dusty-pink brocade-like cloth and lace. A large framed photograph taken on their wedding day hung above Primo's side of the bed. Like all colour photographs processed in the 1970s, it had faded to a dull pinky-brown and had a soft romantic quality to it. Primo and his beautiful bride posed in the centre of the wedding party, with his father and aunt on one side, and Pasquale's parents on the other. Around them stood a large group of friends and the rabbi, immortalized in their laughter of the moment. On the left, behind a low wall, clustered a group of ragged street people. If one looked closely at the photograph, Pasquale, wearing a well-cut suit, could be seen in the background, leaving the group.

When Beatrice lived at home the photograph stood on her dressing table. It was the only thing Primo had moved after she left.

The lounge of number 21 served as Primo's study. Here were an armchair, upholstered in Sanderson linen, a typist's chair and a desk piled with books and journals. Bookshelves lined the walls. Crystals hanging at the window caught the late-afternoon sun, splintering it into rainbows.

The room that Primo's aunt had used as a pantry on the 21 side was now his consulting room. Its window, which looked onto the well-trafficked Kloof Street, was curtained in red velvet. Two chairs faced each other across a round table on which were placed a crystal ball and a pack of Tarot cards.

Wrought-iron sconces, holding ten candles each, hung on two of the walls.

On this side of the house there was another locked room that no one ever entered.

Primo's father and aunt, having given Primo a wonderful though somewhat isolated and eccentric childhood, decided, when he reached his mid-twenties and manhood, to die. They felt, when he married Beatrice – whom they had known since she was a little girl, and whom they loved dearly – that their earthly duty to him was done and their reason for living fulfilled. They believed that in death their nightmares would end.

As far as Primo could establish, his father and aunt had just lain down, each on their own bed, and died. They left no notes and there was no violence in their dying. Their deaths, appearing to have been simply a quiet planned falling into deep and eternal sleep, were a great shock to Primo. It had never occurred to him that they would not live to a ripe old age. Also, because they had died together and without explanation, he felt betrayed, abandoned and angry.

Newly married and living in Beatrice's flat, Primo had come to visit them on the afternoon of their deaths, as he did every day. It was bright and wintry (he remembered the shaft of sunlight on his aunt's alabaster-like face). The house was filled with the ticking and gonging of his father's clocks. Not finding his father in the front workshop, he glanced in his bedroom and thought that the still figure, lying on his back, a crocheted blanket across his legs, his hands folded across the chest, a light smile on his lips, was merely asleep.

How unlike his father, Primo had thought, to take a nap. He made his way to the combined kitchen. As usual the table was laid in readiness for his visit and afternoon coffee: cups and saucers set out on the embroidered tablecloth, a plateful of home-made brioche covered with a lace doily, a pot of his aunt's mulberry jam, a jug of whipped cream, sugar cubes in the bowl. There was no hint of anything untoward, though normally at this time of day his aunt would have been in the back yard tending her garden, and there would certainly have been something good simmering on the stove.

Primo walked down the second passage to the room he had shared with his aunt and which, since his marriage, was now her own. His aunt was lying on her bed in exactly the same position as his father. Now Primo realized something was wrong.

'Zia Lidia,' he whispered from the doorway, and again, louder, 'Zia Lidia.' But she did not stir. Her face, white and still, the shaft of winter sunlight accentuating its morbidity, frightened him.

He walked back to his father's room and stood at the bedside. His father's eyes were not fully closed. Primo touched his cold forehead, noticing white dry saliva at the edge of his lips, and felt ill.

After the inquest – which revealed nothing – and the funeral, Primo locked and never again entered the bedroom he had shared with his aunt. He locked his father's workshop and left the many clocks to run down, so the rhythmic sounds of time passing, which Primo had known throughout his life, grew silent.

He decided, with Beatrice, to move back home. After gutting his aunt's pantry on the 21 side and transforming it into a consulting room, they repainted the entire house and refurnished his father's bedroom. Beatrice bought new linen and hung up the two Pre-Raphaelite reproductions. Then they got on with life together, with much sadness at first, for there was an emptiness now, without the old people. Beatrice mourned them as much as Primo did for theirs had been like a second home to her.

When she left him for Pasquale, Beatrice had not given Primo warning either, and the pattern of her leaving had a disturbing resonance. He had just returned from the Namib desert – where he had gone to buy crystals – and found her gone. Unlike his father and aunt, she had taken some of her clothes. Like them, she left no note of explanation. Instead she had told him, when he phoned looking for her (at exactly seven in the morning – he remembered this small detail), that she was with Pasquale. It was as simple as that. What he could not remember was whether she had said for how long she would be away, or why she had left him, or whether he had done her wrong. All this was erased by the tsunami of emotions that overwhelmed him as he put down the phone.

Abandoned again, he had sat at the kitchen table and cried.

The community to which Primo, Beatrice and Pasquale belonged was a mixed one, but its core consisted of Italians and Jews who ran small businesses in Long Street, between Wale Street and the Buitensingel intersection leading to Kloof Street. It was a close-knit community of traders, financiers and restaurateurs whose parents had left Europe before or after World War II and sailed to Cape Town. They had set up shops and businesses (living upstairs) in a Long Street which was at the time run-down and not as fashionable as it would become in later years (though it would always retain a seedy side).

Long Street, lined by double-storeyed Victorian buildings, some classic and some modernized, had always been busy and noisy, but over the years the focus and content of its shops, and the type of businesses that operated from it, changed. Sack General Dealer, once a housewife's paradise of kitchen utensils and haberdashery, was now Sack Antiques. Stern News Agency was now Stern Cartographer and here one could find, among the files and boxes of yellowed maps of worlds once unknown, ancient Portuguese navigational charts of the coasts of Africa, salvaged from the ruined libraries of Angola. Solomon's Pawn Shop had evolved into Solomon Financial Services. Biccari Jewellers, which dealt primarily in diamonds, had its beginnings in scrap metals. Only Baldinger's Apothecary had not changed and, with its late-Edwardian interior and collection of original jars and tubs, was now a veritable museum of pharmaceutical dispensing. It was run by Alexia, the wife of Dr Adam Baldinger.

There were more restaurants than in the old days, and the clubs that had opened in the late 1940s to cater for ex-servicemen were now up-market and attracted professionals and high earners. A heady cosmopolitan atmosphere was generated by the genteel Maginty's Cigar Bar, the lively Bregman's Afrika that served West African cuisine, the serene vegetarian restaurant, Emerich's Bliss, and the warm, passionate Da Pasquale. These restaurants stood in line with Tafelberg Bottle Store, Clarke's Antiquarian Bookshop and Romana Florist, across the road from Sissy-and-Esquire (a clothing and body-decor emporium) and Stairway to Paradise, a brothel run by Pasquale's sister, Virginia.

Some of the upstairs apartments had been converted to backpacker lodges and drew many young foreign tourists to the area. These travellers were occasionally mugged and robbed, for, though this part of Cape Town was trendy and wealthy, gangs of street children and vagrants roamed here too, as did criminals and a host of illegal immigrants trying to wrest control of the vibrant drug trade from local merchants.

Although Primo and Pasquale were deeply fond of each other and had been close since childhood, theirs was, on the face of it, an unlikely friendship. They both loved poetry and philosophical debate, but where Primo was a quiet, introspective, rather shy person, Pasquale was passionate, volatile, noisy and energetic. Pasquale drank too much, while Primo never touched alcohol.

They were both striking in their looks – tall, well-built and attractive to women. Though Pasquale used this to his advantage, Primo gave it no attention. Pasquale dressed elegantly, chose his clothes well, had a personal tailor, enjoyed his body, fragranced himself with expensive colognes, always took note of his reflection when passing a mirror; Primo dressed conservatively and modestly in linen suits, or cargo pants with plain cotton shirts, his only break in style being the purple velvet cloak he wore while consulting.

As adolescents, just out of school, they had been conscripted to the army and served together in Angola, where they were exposed to the frank horror of war. Here their innocence was shattered and the idyllic world of their young lives splintered before their eyes. War came upon them as a great and marauding slayer of everything good, sparing them nothing of its brute demeanour, hiding none of its harsh truths. It wounded their spirits and scarred them each deeply and indelibly, though differently. They would carry these markings for the rest of their days – Pasquale occasionally violently reliving the horrors he had been exposed to, Primo internalizing and suffering over them.

P asquale adventured through many romantic liaisons and affairs, but Primo did not. Nor did he give much thought to love and relationships, seeming not to notice when women flattered him and so never responding to their flirtations. Until one day, browsing in Sack Antiques, he came across a reproduction of Dante Gabriel Rossetti's *Beata Beatrix* and, seeing in it a beautiful and haunting resemblance to the real Beatrice, felt a new deep emotion stir within himself, and realized that he loved her.

Primo bought the painting, and another, Evelyn de Morgan's *Aurora Triumphans*, not because the subjects of this second picture showed any resemblance to Beatrice, but because he found the three angels it portrayed beguiling. He had both wrapped and ribboned, and invited Beatrice to meet him at the third bench in Government Avenue, where, under the oaks and watched by squirrels, he presented them to her and asked her to marry him.

He knew that Beatrice and Pasquale were lovers, but he also knew that Pasquale made love to many others and that he had no intention of ever marrying Beatrice. Primo's proposal was well planned and rehearsed. He intended to recite, in Latin, the poem *De Acme et Septimio* by Gaius Catullus, for he believed that none of the ancient poets had captured so true an image of the passionate devotion and ecstasy of lovers as had his favourite bard in this poem. He would recite it, then translate it, then take Beatrice's hand and slip onto her finger a ring fashioned – by the jeweller Biccari – from antique Russian silver and an aquamarine.

That was his plan, but, under the oaks, Primo's inherent shyness trapped his song of love. All he managed was to take Beatrice's hands and ask, 'Would you like to share your life with me? Would you like to marry me?'

Completely taken aback at his proposal, and later wincing at how she had ruined the romance of the moment, Beatrice asked, 'What will Pasquale say?'

'But you're not still going out together. You're good friends, not lovers.'

'No, we're not. I mean, yes, we are. Not lovers. Friends. Sissy Plumb is his love of the moment. So it's really over with us – physically, I mean. I suppose ours wasn't a proper relationship – always on and off. He's more of a brother, isn't he?'

Primo took her face in his hands and kissed her

mouth. 'Marry me, Beatrice,' he said. 'I'll love you and cherish you for as long as I live.'

On the afternoon of Primo's marriage proposal, and while he and Beatrice strolled arm in arm through the oaks, Pasquale was in his kitchen stirring up a *salsa pizzaiola*, humming alongside Bizet's *Carmen* and reflecting, as he crushed garlic and chopped origanum, on the versatility of the humble tomato. Had he but asked Primo to read his Tarot spread, he might have had forewarning of what was to come. But he was a man who lived confidently in the moment, and never enquired into his future.

Later that night, as Primo was about to fall asleep, he realized that he had forgotten to give his betrothed her ring. He dressed hurriedly and ran all the way to her flat, where, now fired with a sense of romance and chivalry, he shouted up to her to come out onto the balcony. She stood on the veranda, all lit up by flashing neons, her hair rippling in the wind, her long white nightgown picking up the lurid colours of the pulsing 7Eleven lights.

'Will you marry me?' he shouted above the roar of the traffic, his unbuttoned linen shirt blown open by the wind, his chest glistening as the lights around him shone on its film of sweat. 'I have a ring!' He held it up. 'Chests of diamonds and rubies! And a castle with a moat! And fine weavings to wrap you in! And fields of *fynbos*! And a small orchestra to play at your bidding! All for you! If you marry me!'

Street people gathered around him, looking up at

the beautiful woman he was calling to, cheering her
and offering him drinks of meths and cheap wine.
He ran to the security gate as it clicked open, then
bounded up the stairs to her second-floor apartment
to find Beatrice on the landing, laughing like a
delighted young girl. He fell to his knees, took her
hand and slipped the ring onto her finger.

'Come inside,' she said, touching his hair as he
knelt before her.

'No, my lady. I won't enter your chambers until
you are my wife,' he replied, walking backwards
into the lift and bowing as the doors closed.

When he got back home, breathless with joy, his
father and aunt were waiting, in their pyjamas, on
the stoep. He lifted his aunt into his arms and
swung her round so her plait whipped the air
and her laughter and protests rang out.

'Beloved son,' said his father. 'We wish joyous life
for you both.'

'We have nothing to give Beatrice,' lamented
Lidia, distractedly doing up Primo's buttons. 'I have
nothing belonging to our family. Not our mother's
ring, not our mother's gold chain, not our mother's
bracelets. The Gestapo took everything.'

Eugenio put his arm around his sister's shoulders.
'You must tell Beatrice about our mother's jewels.
Just describe them to her, so she has the picture
in her mind of what should be hers now, as the
betrothed of our son. And tomorrow we will call
the jeweller Biccari to fashion something especially

for you to give her. Come, let me get you paper and pencil and you can draw the chain our mother wore, so he makes an exact copy. He is young and talented and he'll make a true replica, of this I'm certain. But let's first go in and celebrate. Was that cake I smelt baking earlier? Have you baked a cake, Lidia? Then let's eat it now. It's such a beautiful night, we can sit out at the back.'

Father and son escorted Lidia inside, arm in arm with her in the middle, smiling over her head at each other.

In her flat, Beatrice sat before the two paintings Primo had given her. Yes, she agreed, there was a resemblance between the Beatrix of the Rossetti picture and herself. And the three angels of the second, as Primo had pointed out, were utterly beautiful and brought with them a powerful and wondrous quality of light and darkness. She kissed Primo's engagement ring. 'I'll love and cherish you too, Primo. For as long as I live,' she whispered.

Primo courted Beatrice with old-fashioned gentility, not making love to her until their first night of marriage, in her Overbeek apartment, with the neon lights of Long Street flashing on and off and streaking through the bedroom. He had arranged with Romana Florist to fill the flat with roses. The bed was strewn with marigold petals and lavender.

That Primo was virginal and unskilled was not

40

a problem, for Beatrice, young as she was, was no stranger to the territory he had not yet entered, having been introduced to it by Pasquale while still at school. Primo explored her body with a tenderness much like that of walking through an unspoilt field of flowering disas, or touching the leaves of pelargoniums to release their subtle fragrance.

Beatrice was dressed for the wedding by Sissy Plumb of Sissy-and-Esquire in a gown of raw silk beaded across the bodice with tiny pearls. She wore her long hennaed hair loose, threaded through with fresh jasmine. All the Long Street community came to their wedding, which was conducted by Rabbi Steinberg but held in the garden of the Lutheran church at the top of Long Street (to the consternation of the Rabbinical Council). Lazar played gypsy music that spun its way through the branches of cypress trees, around the church steeple and out into the traffic, where it was soon overpowered, but not before it moved hearts and made guests reflect on passion and beauty.

Primo's father and aunt, both deeply shy, walked arm in arm, and sent a ripple of interest through the crowd of guests, for they were dressed in postwar attire (highly fashionable at the time they were last worn, but now quaintly *démodé*). Lidia had on a beige striped suit, its jacket elegantly cut with padded shoulders, the below-knee-length skirt slit seductively at the back. She walked in high chunky shoes and on her head wore a coquettish beret

41

with a pheasant's feather, dulled by time, sweeping elegantly across it. Eugenio's suit was also striped, with turn-up trousers and a close-fitting jacket. Had they been strolling through a park in 1950, they would have cut a dash.

Primo bought dozens of sugar buns and Cokes for the street children, and a crate of beer and flagons of wine for Long Street's paupers and lumpens who joined in the revelry with relish. They were soon drunk, brawling and incoherent outside the church walls, or leaning over the gate making pronouncements on Beatrice's beauty and the generosity of her new husband: 'Hey! Miss Beatrice! You got yourself a good man. And Mr Primo! You got a *lekker* good woman. And Mr Primo! Thanks for the party, hey. This is a *lekker* party. Hey! Mr Lazar! You play so sweet on that fiddle, man. As true's God.'

When Beatrice had told Pasquale she was going to marry Primo, he did not immediately react. They had grown up together and been friends for ever – they would always be friends. She had worked for him since he opened Da Pasquale, first waitressing, and then at the bar. She was part of his family and life.

Only when he saw her in her wedding gown, at Primo's side, dazzlingly beautiful under the pink oleander and embraced by the blue plumbago of the garden, laughing as Primo whispered a tenderness, did he realize that there would now be a shift in the dynamic of their relationship. He had lost the woman he cared for more than any other, to his best friend.

Pasquale left the wedding early and went home to drink. On his balcony, a bottle of *grappa* in hand, he worked himself into a state of anger and anguish at his foolish lack of foresight. Cursing his immaturity and stupidity, he decided to kill himself. He took a pistol to Signal Hill, planning to blow his heart out in the eucalyptus forest that still grew there at the time. But he couldn't pull the trigger. Instead he went to his sister's newly opened brothel, intending to lie with all her prostitutes, one after another without stopping, until he died from exertion and loss of body fluid. But he couldn't do this either. For the first time in his young life, his libido failed him and he could not service even one of Virginia's ladies. So he drank and wept and became violent, throwing bottles around and smashing tables.

Virginia called an ambulance and he spent a good two weeks in the Volks hospital, sedated. His parents sat at his bedside, day in and day out, dozing off now and then, wiping his forehead, whispering to each other. 'We should have encouraged him to propose to Beatrice years ago – after he finished in the army,' said his father. 'Yes,' agreed his mother. 'But there is nothing to be done now.'

*   *   *

43

hen Pasquale recovered, he invited Primo and Beatrice to dinner. He closed the delicatessen to other patrons and laid on a feast of *parmigiana di melanzane alla Calabrese*, *tortellini alla Romagnola* and *agnello alla pastora*. He asked Lazar to play from the top of the stairs, so as not to be seen and to give a sense that an angel's music filled the restaurant that night.

They ate till the early hours, Pasquale and Beatrice drinking wine, Primo content with mineral water. For dessert Pasquale offered them *miele e ricotta*. 'To wish us a continuing sweet life together,' he said, smiling into Beatrice's eyes.

When it was time to leave, Pasquale saw his friends to the door. Heady on Villiera Chenin Blanc and not quite steady on his feet, he announced, 'I'm going to fetch you back one day, my Beatrice. I'll come on a white stead, a horse with bells tied to its mane, clip-clop, clip-clop, up Kloof Street and I'll bring you back here to live upstairs, above my shop . . . No! Don't laugh! Watch out for that, my Primo, my best beloved friend. I will fetch your wife, my lover. You must keep watch over her day and night. Remember, she was mine long before she was yours. Now, goodnight. Let me go and feed Lazar. He must be starving.'

They had all three laughed that night, at the door of Da Pasquale in Long Street, as good friends laugh, and felt pleased with their friendship. Had Primo but once thrown his own Tarot spread, he might have had some forewarning of the truth concealed in jest.

Pasquale never married. Instead he devoted most of his energies to his profession and at the same time conducted one affair after another, unable and unwilling to commit himself to anyone. Beatrice remained his only woman friend and continued to work at the bar of Da Pasquale. As the years passed he confided in her more and more and his love of her matured. This never troubled or threatened Primo and never gave rise to jealousy. And because Pasquale also loved and admired Primo, the friendship triangle remained a complex and enduring one.

The Long Street crowd were city people who had no experience of natural wilderness, though they occasionally picnicked on Table Mountain. None of them, except Primo, had any understanding of unspoilt nature. His psyche alone bore the illuminations of the unblemished earth, and these he had garnered from the Angolan savannah and a single visit to Zululand when the police had asked him to track down a kidnapped baby.

His intuitions and visions had led him to a remote area of forest where the small limbless body was buried in a shallow grave, the victim of a *muti*-murder. Primo had found the body within the first few hours of the day, but he asked the detectives who escorted him whether they would remain with him through the night until the next morning, so that he might walk through the forest. A sense of otherness had woken in him, under the great canopy of tangled branches, and he wanted to stay with it for a while longer.

It was a sand forest surrounded by woodland, and what inscribed itself on his heart was its sacredness. He did not recognize the trees, could not name the lala palms and monkey oranges, nor the silver cluster leaves and the velvet bush willows. The black thorns too bore no name. But all of them together, tousled and entwined and bound by vines, decorated with orchids, informed his sensitivity, so he could ever after close his eyes and feel poetry within him.

It was this poetry that fuelled his love of Beatrice, this quiet earthly meeting of words which could never be spelt out or written but which murmured and sighed the way wind did through the last of the Zululand forests.

In the month that Primo travelled to the Namib desert to buy crystals from the goatherds who roamed the rocky outcrops, the planets Mercury, Venus, Mars, Jupiter and Saturn formed a peculiar conjunction, all clustered together and visible to the naked eye – even in Cape Town's bright sky.

Coincidentally, on the second Saturday night of

that month, at the regular Da Pasquale poker game, an unusual and recurring hand was played: the dealer repeatedly put down the same five cards. This happened regardless of who shuffled or dealt. The players, all seasoned and skilled gamblers, were amazed and perplexed by this, for none, in their long careers, had ever experienced such a phenomenon. Dr Baldinger attributed it to the energies of the planetary pageant that adorned the night sky.

'Sack! Have you fixed the pack?' asked Solomon.

'What are you suggesting? That I cheat? I'm a skilled player. You know that. I can swear for my honesty and integrity on the fortune of my shop.'

'Biccari! What are you doing? Have you got cards up your sleeve?'

'Don't insult me. How long have you known me? When have I ever cheated?'

'Is it you, Stern?'

'Are we not principled players? Is that not what has held us together for so many years – our sense of honour and trustworthiness? Please, do me a favour. Why should I now fix a hand?'

'Bregman, what are you up to?'

'Nothing but fair play, and you know that. I'm as amazed as you are at this. Stern's right, we don't need to check one another's honesty. It's there. It always has been.'

'Emerich! Tell me what you know that I don't. Is it you, manipulating behind our backs?'

'I can't believe you suspect any of us. This is just

some weird coincidence, or an outsider is somehow influencing the cards – but there are no strangers here tonight,' answered Emerich, glancing around the delicatessen.

'Romana! Last to answer. What about it?'

'I'll step out now if need be – you'll see this has nothing to do with me. But I'm in agreement with the others. For what to cheat? There's no point in playing if we play dirty. Give me the pack. Let me deal the last game.'

It was two in the morning. Beatrice, Pasquale and Dr Baldinger stood around the players. Everyone was quiet.

Romana shuffled twice and dealt two cards to each. The players noiselessly pushed their bets to the centre of the table and waited tentatively as, one at a time and slowly, she dealt another three cards, face up, in the centre of the table.

The ten of hearts.

'No! Surely not again?' she said.

The jack of hearts.

'Impossible!' said Biccari, under his breath.

The queen of hearts.

'No! This is ridiculous,' whispered Solomon.

The players and those watching took deep breaths. No one spoke.

'Last two cards, guys,' said Romana, forcing a calmness to her voice as she broke the silence. 'Anyone betting?'

She waited. Biccari and Solomon put their money

down. She slowly peeled back the top card and placed it for all to see.

The king of hearts.

'What the hell is going on? This is ridiculous!' said Stern.

Then she dealt the last card.

It was the joker.

'Damn misdeal! Again!' exclaimed Bregman, slamming the table. 'Where does this damn joker keep coming from? Someone keeps feeding it into the pack.'

Emerich loosened his tie and stood up. With his hands in his pockets he looked down at the spread of cards.

Sack swung round to face Pasquale and, with an accusing look, asked, 'Are you the joker to-night, Pasqui? Have you got something to do with this?'

Pasquale burst out laughing. 'Me? Tell me, Sack, how do I get near your cards?'

'It's the planets,' soothed Dr Baldinger. 'Five planets. Five recurring cards, one of them an intrusive rogue – the joker.'

'Pour us Chivas Regal, Beatrice, please,' said Solomon. 'Nothing else. Neat. No ice. Then we're going home. This is unsettling. What a night!'

'Make it double tots, Beatrice,' said Pasquale. 'On the house.'

The players all stood. They knocked back their drinks, grimaced, and bade each other goodnight.

With a puzzled frown, Dr Baldinger turned to Beatrice and asked, 'Shall I walk you home, Beatrice? When will Primo be back?'

'In about three weeks. We've still got to cash up. Pasquale will walk me back, thanks.'

'Well, goodnight, then. Goodnight, Pasquale.'

'Goodnight.'

Pasquale drew the blinds after his waiters had left, and switched off all but the lights over the bar. Beatrice cashed up and locked the day's takings in the safe at the back.

'Come, Beatrice, let's go. Don't leave your jacket.'

In years to come, Beatrice would look back on this night and ask whether there had indeed been something at play, some force that nudged her and Pasquale at the door so that they brushed against each other, then touched each other, then held each other's hands.

Pasquale took her by the shoulders and, though she stiffened momentarily, she offered no resistance when he kissed first her hair, then her brow, then her lips, which, though he had wanted to, he had not kissed for twenty years. 'Beatrice,' he whispered. 'Don't go back to your empty house. Stay with me tonight.'

A motorcyclist whined up Long Street. The lights of the bar danced on the bottled colours of bourbon, Sabra, Amarula, Johnny Walker and Dom Pedro, and shone back from the bevelled mirror behind them.

At that self same moment, under the Namib sky, Primo, in his sleeping bag, looked up at the abundance of stars – milk spilt across the blackness, with five planets clustered in a group, like angels gathered there, discussing something. Primo realized that if he were in space somewhere, looking back, he would see six in the group, for the earth too would be visible in the cluster, with the moon humbly among them.

He lay awake until the dawn, which, as though it were a paintbrush, drew a line of red across the horizon. A lone bat-eared fox barked close by.

Pasquale lived above his delicatessen, and it was to this apartment that he led Beatrice, up the ornate but narrow Burmese teak staircase at the far end of the shop, as though he were leading her back into the time of their childhood friendship and adolescent love. As Beatrice would later reflect, she had not planned to betray Primo, or hurt him, or leave him, for that matter. This was merely an impulsive moment of play while he was away. She had no intention of staying with Pasquale more than that one night.

The apartment was a spacious and tastefully furnished bedsitting room, with a double bed and sumptuous silk and brocade bedding. Persian carpets covered the floor and two deep black leather couches were festooned with richly coloured silk cushions. On the walls hung a number of original oil paintings – some very valuable (Pasquale owned an Irma Stern) – and a carved Zanzibarian door. At the end of the bed stood an inlaid rosewood table.

The large bathroom, fitted in the 1950s, had, in its centre, a ball-and-claw tub with brass taps, a pedestal washbasin and an original Victorian water closet decorated with cherubs and pink roses. An Afghan kelim served as a bath mat. Against one of the walls stood two ornate Louis XIV armoires. A carved, ivory inlaid kist had been placed under a huge gilt-framed mirror salvaged from the lobby of some demolished, now forgotten, hotel in Uitenhage.

Pasquale lit two large candles and a bedside lamp, threw open the balcony doors and drew the white muslin curtains closed so they billowed slightly in the light breeze. He put on a cassette of Paganini's 24 Caprices and turned to face Beatrice.

Holding her gaze, he took off his clothes, then came towards her with his arms open. He ran his hands through her thick hair and began to undress her, undoing her fastenings, kissing her arms, pulling her garments from her, dropping everything to her feet. She had merely to step from them, like a birthing Venus, into his arms.

Pasquale led her to the bed and spread her out on the red silk cover, then stepped back, gazing at her naked body for a moment. He lay down next to her, running a hand across each breast, kissing her stomach.

'I will make love to you slowly and with deliberation, mistress,' he said, and laughed. 'I will inflame your beautiful form as it yields to my hands. Here on my own bed I have the softness of your flesh, of your skin, of your hair . . . How is this possible? You are forbidden fruit. You are the wife of my best friend. You are the only woman I adore.

'Why did you leave me, my cherished one? Why did you marry Primo?' he asked, biting against her fingers as she tried to hold his lips closed, to stop him from saying more, then kissing her mouth with tenderness. 'I love you, Beatrice,' he whispered at her ear.

Beatrice could feel the wetness of his skin against hers, and remembered their youthful love and the play of their bodies. His hands, as he explored her now, seemed never to have forgotten her, though her body was no longer that of the girl she had been. They remembered everything of her body's landscape, traversing it as though they had mapped it only yesterday.

'You have not changed,' he whispered, and she could taste his tears. 'You have not changed and you have not aged, and I know you as my own. I will recite you poems, if you want: I can recite Neruda and Tennyson while I make love, as I used to. But I can also be silent, so you can just listen to my heart bursting inside me.'

Afterwards, they lay together for a while, aware that they had crossed some invisible line, and that nothing would ever be the same again. The Paganini cassette had reached its end. The traffic outside offered in its place an awkward music.

Pasquale got up, opened a bottle of wine and poured them each a glass. Then he ran the bath for her, adding essential oils to the water, so the mixed fragrances of neroli, bergamot and carnation rose in the steam, permeating the room. He tied Beatrice's hair back into a knot.

'Don't close the door, Beatrice,' he said as she went through to the bathroom. 'Bathe with it open.'

He replayed Paganini and cocooned himself in the covers while Beatrice lay in the hot water. A shudder of emotion seized him and he began to cry. But the frantic passages of the violin filling the apartment wrapped up the sounds of his weeping, so Beatrice did not hear.

She did not go home the next day.

They made love often, after that first night, in the weeks that Primo was still away, and Pasquale paid great attention to the detail of his lovemaking. For him, love and sex should be art forms, like cooking. He believed that, if love was a central component, one couldn't just mix the ingredients of a woman's body with a man's without some thought, some preparation. So he approached the pleasuring of Beatrice, the excitement of their orgasm, the tenderness after their passion, in the same way he did the presentation of a thoughtfully made *zabaglione*, or *budino Toscano*.

In contrast, it never occurred to Primo – sensitive though he was – to *prepare* to make love, to soften the lighting, to sprinkle the linen with rose-water, to place on Beatrice's tongue a fragrant *amaretto*, no larger than an almond in its shell. This Pasquale did. And, because Pasquale was a lover and not a husband, he was aware that at any moment his beloved would be reclaimed, or want to go home. So every instant of love became, like the last moment of life itself, a treasure.

Whenever he and Beatrice were to make love, Pasquale would have ready a bottle of Thelema Sauvignon Blanc in an ice bucket and a Kanonkop Pinotage wrapped in a starched linen serviette, cork off and breathing, as well as a pewter platter of good things to eat – sometimes mini garlic pizzas and thin slices of *cotechino*, or slices of oven-bronzed pitta bread with sardines and origanum; sometimes simply fragrant biscuits redolent with rosemary.

He undressed her. 'I like to unwrap you – you're my gift to myself; I like to release you – you're a butterfly inside a pupa,' he told her. He kept a pile of poetry books and various collected works at the side of the bed and would read from them to tantalize her with the achings and musings of lovers who had captured in words that which he longed to.

Their lovemaking was fuelled by Pasquale's passion for life, by his volatile explosive moods, by his love of Beatrice's ample rounded form and by his desperate jealous need to reclaim the past and fill it with their togetherness. He wanted to halt time in its movement, to stall the present, so he and Beatrice could remain for ever within this cusp, in which Primo was away and the two of them were together. It was lovemaking tempered by Beatrice's soft quiet nature, and was marred only by the fact that they both loved Primo.

ne night, shortly before Primo was due back, after they had closed the delicatessen and were upstairs lying on the bed, Pasquale teased, 'Beatrice, if Botero lived in this town he would ask you to model for him. I can just see you as his Colombiana eating an apple, or his Donna undressing herself.'

'Are you saying I'm fat, Pasqui? His models are obese.'

'No. No. I don't mean to say you're fat. Yes. His models are obese. No. I just mean his style, his style. He paints so voluptuously. His women's curves are so like yours. There's more flesh to them, I admit. But the *feel* of their bodies that he captures – that feel is yours, my precious rounded one.'

'They're not very pretty.'

'No. Pretty they are not. They look like the whores who work for my sister. I've told you – I'm talking *feel*. They feel like you. Your beauty, he hasn't captured. That's why he'd need you as a model – to introduce your loveliness to his canvases.'

He took a handful of her hair and began to plait it, becoming pensive and saying, 'I want to tell you something, Beatrice. During all these years that you've been married to Primo, when I slept with others, it was always with my eyes closed. Literally. In my mind I always saw you. You must believe this. I never wanted other women's bodies. I only used them. In my soul I made love to you. I remembered every part of you. Your body remained in my mind like a painting hung before me.'

Beatrice said nothing. She could sense where he was heading, and did not want to follow.

'It's been hard for me, all these years, to have you so near me, working with me, being such a close friend, yet not mine,' he continued. 'Part of me was content to have you almost at my side, enjoying my life with me, almost completely part of me, almost mine. Primo could have moved away with you to another town; he could have taken you to Spain, or North Africa or anywhere, and then I would not have had you, as I have, as my wonderful and good friend. But I wanted more. I've always wanted more. I've wanted all of you. Can you understand this?'

Still Beatrice said nothing.

'Do you think of me, Beatrice, when you lie with Primo? Or did you just forget my body throughout all these twenty years? Tell me. Do you ever think of me when your husband makes love to you?'

'Don't ask these questions, Pasqui. Primo and I have a good strong marriage – you know that. And we are good strong friends, the three of us. You're just going to work yourself into a jealous mood. Don't, please.'

'I'm jealous already. I've always been jealous. So tell me at least that I'm better than Primo. Tell me that my body is firmer, stronger, sexier; that I satisfy you more than he does. Tell me, Beatrice,' he said, pinning her arms down and biting at her neck. 'I want to hear you say it because I know he doesn't make love like I do.'

'Stop it, Pasqui. Or I'll go home!' she said laughing, trying to break loose.

'No! I'll shoot myself if you leave me again. I'll stand in my bar and shoot myself publicly. Then I'll come back and haunt you. I'll pull at your legs while you lie in bed and smear them with syrup. I'll throw rum babas at you from heaven every time Primo touches you!'

'Do you think there's a place for you in heaven, Pasqui?'

'Of course! I'll cook for God. He's sick already of milk and honey. Now come, my darling. Lie back. Relax. Open yourself to me. I won't ask you again. But one day you'll tell me, of your own accord. One day you'll tell me that you missed me, and that you made a mistake leaving me, and that Primo can't make love to save his life. You'll write me a poem and I'll wear it stapled to my heart until I die.'

In her brothel, Stairway to Paradise, Pasquale's sister re-created the atmosphere of a nineteenth-century bordello, costuming her ladies – among them two dwarfs – in corsets, suspenders, lace stockings and seductive gowns. Heavily perfumed and made up, they lounged invitingly in the deep armchairs of the salon or at the bar, fluttering false eyelashes and pursing red lips.

Like her brother, Virginia was emotional, impulsive and drank too much. Like him too, she was a perfectionist in her work and had amassed a small fortune, for her brothel generally served only the rich and famous. A true artist, she had defied the insipid laws of segregation during the apartheid years and refused to separate people by colour.

'Beauty is colour!' she challenged her more reserved clients. 'And inside, believe me, is all the same.'

Virginia mixed her staff carefully, as though on a palette, employing those with skins of black and brown, pale whites and toffee browns, mustards, ivory and pearl. These she offset against gaudy and strident decor so that entering her brothel, with its gold ceilings, its emerald, ruby and topaz walls, its windows draped in gold chiffon, was like stepping into an oil painting peopled with striking big-bosomed women. She was never harassed for contravening the Immorality Act, because among her brothel's regular patrons were some highly placed ministers and their deputies.

She had scoured South Africa to find two dwarfs prepared to service men who were bored with the ordinary. On one of her explorations she found the metre-high Lillian Meintjies of Ficksburg. Lillian was the youngest daughter of the postmaster and lived a lonely life, crocheting baby jackets and booties to sell at the local home-industry bazaar. She had spent most of her life indoors avoiding people, not from shame, but through a lack of pride. Virginia changed all this when she employed her. With her hair permed and dyed red, a tattooed spider on her rump, whips and a leather jerkin, Lillian was in great demand at Stairway to Paradise.

Virginia found Sara Kloppers, who stood just a little taller than Lillian and had a poorly re-constructed harelip, in Caledon. Here she had earned her keep as a scullery hand at the Brazzaville Bar. Sara was more than happy to change pro-fession and, like Lillian, settled into Virginia's pleasure house with great delight. The Little Ladies, as they came to be known, their breasts bursting against boned lace corsets, their navels adorned with rings, often worked together, pleasuring a client simultaneously.

Virginia employed the dwarfs because she was drawn to the unusual. 'There is beauty in what is conventionally thought ugly,' she pronounced. 'Those stumpy little bodies! They are just like scarab beetles, quite as lovely!' She encouraged Sara to wear an amethyst stud through her disfigured lip. 'Why cover it up, Saratjie? Enhance it!'

Virginia herself serviced only one client, Dr Cloete van Rensburg, a plastic surgeon who visited her private apartment, on the top floor of the brothel, a few evenings each week. She loved him and believed that theirs was not a professional relationship, but one true and deep, though it was not. He always paid for her services, but, because she refused to accept money, he put it in the top drawer of her dressing table, which was by now very full.

Cloete was younger than she and still a maverick at heart, one who enjoyed club life and his freedom. He did not want to commit himself to any long-term relationship or to have children, yet. He felt that, though he enjoyed Virginia sexually, they had little in common and he found being in her presence for too long rather stifling. Whenever they made love she wanted him to stay the rest of the night, to sit with her on the balcony and look out over Long Street, across at the stars above Signal Hill. She would have a platter from Da Pasquale set out with wine on her table. Because he did not want the relationship to develop beyond the confines of the top-floor room of Stairway to Paradise, he never took Virginia out and seldom stayed long, preferring to play pool at Starkey's in Green Point or drink at the Stag's Head down in Hope Street. (Cloete did not mix with the Long Street crowd – he was not overly fond of Jews.)

So Virginia would remain on the balcony alone, naked in good weather, clad in a fur coat in winter, drinking wine, watching the moon and stars rise and sometimes set. She did not know that Cloete frequently visited the bed of her friend, Sissy Plumb.

Virginia had been married for a short time – five days to be exact – to Count Cesare de M., a Venetian nobleman and homosexual fifteen years her senior. He lived with his devoted and demanding mother in a restored *palazzo* overlooking the Canale della Giudecca in Venice. They had met on a *vaporetto* while Virginia, just out of art school, was holidaying in Venice to study the city's masterpieces. It was a chilly day and the colours of the canal water were blends of deep grey and aluminium. Tiny raindrops had settled like clusters of translucent pearls on Virginia's Titian hair and lambswool coat. She looked beautiful. With hindsight she would realize she also looked vulnerable, because he played a mean hand, the Count, enthralling her with his charm and intelligence, romancing her on gondolas and in candle-lit restaurants, accompanying her to galleries and churches and showing her how the quality of light had been variously interpreted by different artists.

They married in a civil ceremony with his mother the only guest, and planned to spend the following months in Cape Town before settling in Venice. However, the Count did not consummate their five-day marriage and this confused Virginia, who made no demands because she was young and rather in awe of him. For their last night in Venice she ordered dinner to be brought up to their room, hoping to arouse him with candlelight and romantic ambience. They were staying in the presidential suite of their hotel, where one of the Count's young boy-lovers worked as a waiter. This young man, by some fateful coincidence, happened to be the one assigned to bring dinner to their room that night.

He arrived bearing a platter of dressed trout and vegetables *sotto olio*. This he placed on a table in the centre of the room, along with two plates, cutlery, wine glasses and serviettes.

Virginia was late in returning from the flower market, for on her way back she had sat on the Accademia Bridge to watch the setting sun darken the colours of the canal. It was early evening when she opened the door of the hotel room.

The Count and his young man did not hear her enter; nor did they hear the door click shut behind her. They became aware of her only when she screamed. As they leapt apart from their embrace,

Virginia threw the flowers across the room: lilies, irises, roses and baby's breath. She took off her shoes and threw them at her husband.

'*Animale!* You bastard!' she shouted.

'No! No! It's nothing! *Calmati! Sta calma! Ti prego!*' he petitioned, his arms outstretched towards Virginia, who picked up the tray of dressed trout and hurled it at him, narrowly missing his head. It crashed through the lead-glass window and sailed out over the pavement below and into the canal.

She pulled her wedding ring from her finger and threw that at him too. It spun through the broken glass, following the trout.

The Count tried to leave the room with some dignity, to explain, to come to some agreement, but this was not possible. He stepped round the flowers, looking stonily ahead. He and the waiter took the service lift to the ground floor and smoked a cigarette in the passage. 'I did it for my mother,' the Count explained to his young friend.

On the black waters of the Canale Grande, bobbing in the wakes of *vaporetti* and motorized gondolas, trailing streamers of mayonnaise, floated the trout, just for a while, before sinking into foul silt.

These were the dramatic five days of Virginia's marriage. She returned to Cape Town, sulked around her brother's delicatessen for a few years, strolled up and down Long Street and the Company Gardens with her ageing parents, sat with them in

De Waal Park, all the while planning a future for herself.

She decided to open a brothel because there had not been one in the city since the Blue Lodge closed down some eight years before. (Whores could hire rooms at the Crown Hotel in Roeland Street, but there was no comfort or classiness involved). She bought the old Meyers Building, had it restored and expensively furnished, and set up for business, targeting rich professionals and high-ranking politicians. She did not return to her maiden name but continued to call herself Contessa Virginia Cesare de M., living upstairs in her brothel, drinking hard and smoking filterless Gauloises. She never healed within herself the hurt of feeling she had been duped and betrayed.

rimo had felt comfortable and secure within his twenty-year marriage to Beatrice. He was a kind, generous husband who never made demands and never quibbled over how she spent his money.

They had reconciled themselves to not having conceived a baby, though Beatrice still sometimes cried about this. She wanted a little girl to dress up and love, and, in the early years of their marriage, bought smocks and chamois-leather booties and a rag doll and kept these in her wardrobe, waiting. She would watch mothers pushing prams through the park, or picnicking under the oaks with their children, and wish for her own. But they never came. Even though she prayed for it, life never took form within her.

Primo had felt comfortable too within their community of friends in the Long Street territory they all frequented and which was the canvas against which he and Beatrice lived out a satisfied life. As a professional soothsayer and magician, he worked long hours, his services being in constant demand. Even so, he and Beatrice socialized a good deal. When she worked at night, he would join her for an hour or so for dinner, eating with her and Pasquale. Then he would go home to read, or study the stars if the night was clear. He would stroll down to fetch her later, stopping for a coffee or a cup of rooibos while she and Pasquale cashed up.

When Beatrice left him, all this changed. She took with her their shared context. The little rituals of their day-to-day living were no longer there for him; nor were their shared habits at home. The pleasures they had enjoyed together of going to City Hall recitals, watching movies at the Labia, browsing the antique shops in New Church Street, strolling Long Street in the evenings, their good times at Da Pasquale, their Saturday nights at the poker games with their philosophical debates and arguments – all these elements of Primo's social stability were now gone. He could not do alone the things they had once done together. He could certainly never look Pasquale in the face again, let alone enter his delicatessen; he had no wish to speak to any of their friends. Primo even let slide his good relationship with Dr Baldinger, and because many of their friends were also his clients, he stopped working.

So as not to meet anyone he knew, Primo avoided Long Street and instead caught taxis into town to shop at OK Bazaars. Rather than take coffee at Da Pasquale – the very thought made his stomach sour – or Maginty's, he would stroll up to the Malay Quarter to eat samoosas and drink sweet mint tea at one of the pavement cafés. Looking out across the city, with the spectacular mountain massif as its backdrop, he would reflect on the pattern of betrayal in his life.

Even his mother, he felt, though her death was untimely and accidental, had betrayed him. For she had left him before he could form memory of her, before he had captured her smells and sentiments and sounds to carry with him through life. He did not have her laughter or her crying or her tenderness in his heart. He had only her absence and his questions of how it would have been to know her.

Primo unplugged the phone and stuck a note on the front door of number 21, advising his clients that he had retired. The note referred people to his apprentice, Beulagh September, who lived in one of the few houses still standing on the edge of District Six, and whom he could recommend with confidence, for she had a sharp clairvoyance.

His sudden retirement caused great consternation and his clients, without considering his wishes, continued to call, hoping he would soon come back to work. They still brought him trays of delicacies, placing them at his door. These he merely stepped over and left for the rats and street people to carry away. His clients would strike the brass knocker (a bat) in desperate disbelief, not accepting the ghastly possibility of having to deal with their future alone. Primo would not answer; rather, he sat in the kitchen or in the lounge or in his study wishing they would go away. Nor did he read the many cards and letters that crammed his postbox.

To stop himself brooding, he turned his attention to the eternally perplexing problem of good and evil. He took from his bookshelves his father's well-thumbed and worn copy of Dante's *Divine Comedy* and, beginning with the 'Inferno', settled down for a long journey through the levels of the Afterlife.

Primo let the household fall apart. Stale breads, mouldy cheeses and withered vegetables cluttered the two *credenze*. Bottles of sour milk and fermenting fruit juices emitted an acrid, lingering smell whenever he opened the fridge. The two sinks were piled with dirty plates, mugs and take-away trays of half-eaten portions. A frying pan coated in congealed rancid oil stood on the stove. A roast chicken, forgotten in the oven, started to putrefy. A vase of dead grey flowers stood

forlornly in the centre of the kitchen table. Primo
did not water the violets that lined the kitchen
windowsills and their leaves drooped. The plants on
the stoep languished with thirst; the back garden
took on a look of neglect as papers and packets,
blown in by the swirling southeast wind, collected
in corners and got caught in the branches of the
mulberry tree. He took to wearing his velvet cloak,
which he had generally worn only when working,
all the time. He let his hair grow long, tying it back
in a thick ponytail.

Sometimes Primo would wake in the night
wanting Beatrice, wanting her closeness and her
body. He missed her warmth and her dream
murmurs. He missed her habit of sometimes in her
sleep reaching over and holding him. So he never
took over the double bed, but continued to sleep on
his side only, expecting her to come back. It was
always a shock, when he woke late at night, to find
her not there. On those occasions he would ease
himself out of bed, open a drawer, fumble for a
handful of her underwear and bury his face in it,
breathing in the fading smell of her perfume.

Then he would throw a dressing-gown over himself, step into his slippers and make his way down
the passage to the kitchen. Here he brewed coffee
and pondered the fate of his marriage, wondering
how it had come about that both Beatrice and
Pasquale had dealt him such a blow. Primo was hurt
that she had left him for a man he now dismissed as

a mere baker, a man who had once been a good friend. No, not merely a good friend, he lamented, a friend who was like a brother. With these sad thoughts he would stare at the patterns on the Bokhara spread across the floor, marvelling at the palette of its colours: deep reds and blues, ivory and yellow ochre, rose and madder. He would ask aloud: 'Whose fingers worked this? Who gathered wild berries and crushed the colours from them? Who composed this pattern?' Then he would turn to his telescope and, focusing on whichever planet was visible between the city buildings, seek solace from deep space.

While looking into the vastness of the outer world, he would caress his wife with his thoughts, hoping they would somehow reach her: Don't leave me for ever. For without you, I have no meaning. Without you, I have nothing to live for, only these walls and furnishings and the emptiness of the night. Come home and I will say nothing. I will ask nothing. I will just hold you, for I love you.

He imagined that in her sleep his lips would touch against her hair; that she would sense him close to her, sense his hand on her breast, or on her thigh, as though they were still lying together, in their own bed, in their own home.

Sometimes he would stand in his garden, under the mulberry tree, and speak into the crisp night air: 'If I imagine myself making love to you, will you feel my body against yours? Will you feel me as I kiss your face, your neck, your thick hair, so like the coat of a wild creature? Will you remember the pleasure my body gave you, the pleasure my hands brought to you? Will you remember how we made love, my dearest?'

Perhaps the shrill cries of seagulls or the whine of traffic would respond to him. Even the sharp lashing curses of a drunk *bergie* might reach his ears. But his wife's voice did not come on the wind, through the lonely night.

Although everyone understood why Primo cut himself off without so much as a good-bye, most thought he was overreacting to Beatrice's affair. They gossiped with passion, but no one stood in judgement. For affairs, it was generally accepted, are like the seasons of spring and summer, bursting with colour and passion, but inevitably running their course and returning to the stable autumn and winter of marriage.

'Everyone has affairs, for goodness' sake,' Alexia Baldinger said to her husband while cashing up one evening. 'Primo, of all people should know this. He must have seen hundreds of *ménages à trois* in his crystal ball. Everyone is always in someone else's wife's bed. Only last week I saw Cloete van Rensburg coming out of Sissy Plumb's place. Isn't he in a relationship with the Contessa?

'And anyway, that triangle between the three of them has always been there. Pasquale was on the

71

scene before Primo was. And Beatrice has always
been free and easy with Pasquale, hasn't she? And
still working for him all these years – I mean,
she's right there all the time, always in his space.
Actually, it's amazing this didn't happen years ago.'

'Alexia,' replied her husband, 'it's not for us
to judge. All I can say is I'm very worried about
Primo. He's disconnected his phone and won't
answer the door. He's just closed himself off. It's not
healthy. I wish he would at least let me in, but he
won't.

'And I had a strange encounter last week. You
know that woman, Beulagh September, the one
who's been studying with Primo? She stopped me in
Loop Street, at the post office, and asked about
Primo with much concern. He keeps coming up
when she visions with her crystal ball. She sees
him, with a bloodied rag tied round blinded eyes
and with a dead albatross tied round his neck,
walking out into the sea, then drowning. She unsettled me – not with what she visioned but with her
anxiety, which matches mine. Not everything these
crystal balls throw up is true. And anyway, she's
still an apprentice. She's not an experienced soothsayer. Primo will never take his life. I know that. I'm
just so concerned about his isolation. He has shut
himself away from all of us. It's not healthy.

'I'll go round tomorrow and try again. Maybe he'll
answer the door. I'll take him some food. I'm sure
he's not eating properly.'

Dr Baldinger helped his wife pull down the blinds and lock the pharmacy. They walked up Bloem Street to their home in the Bo-Kaap, stopping first at Da Pasquale for a cappuccino and a shared slice of *torta nera*.

The human face is a canvas upon which age weathers and defines itself. Across it, time marks its way as it passes, leaving behind a legacy of wrinkles, blemishes and muscle without tone. Virginia's lover, Dr Cloete van Rensburg, became wealthy because women wish to erase these testimonies of time. Though he could not stop the ageing process, he could delay it by cutting away redundant skin sagging beneath the eyes, or by stretching skin back from the face and pinning it to the scalp, beneath the hairline. In this way he surgically stole from time at least ten years of its facial inscription, transforming deep etchings into mere filigree tracings.

Nor did he confine his art to the face. He also sculpted the body form by lifting drooping breasts, or augmenting small ones; he tucked away tummies and trimmed off unflattering folds; he sucked out deposits of fat from thighs, buttocks and even chins.

Cloete was a master of fine suturing; his stitching was careful and precise and one might compare him to an embroiderer, though the threads he used were not cottons and silks dyed to fine colours. His needles were not hand-fashioned from the finest silver, nor were they straight, but curved and made from alloys. They were single-use needles that were thrown away by the hundred, incinerated with bloodied swabs and bits of flesh.

He was a man who, driven by his profession to improve and rejuvenate the human face, had become obsessed with the whole notion of beauty. What is beauty? he wondered. Does it exist at all? Did the perfect face, the well-balanced face portrayed by the Greeks and Romans and later by such masters as Raphael and Michelangelo live only, though eternally, in works of art?

He used the classic faces from these artists' works as the yardstick against which to measure beauty, though he had never come across a living person whose features he considered to be as balanced and aligned. When he looked at a woman's face, even the prettiest, he saw its every imperfection – an eye some millimetres out of alignment with the other; the deepened brow lines on the more expressive side of the face; the irregularity of the nostrils; the too-short distance between the arch of the cheekbones and the jawline.

If the human form is malleable, pliable, mouldable, can its components be worked upon to create perfection? he asked himself. Can I create it? Who were the models the classical artists portrayed? Were they angels, and not human at all? Did angels visit those master artists in the night, and model in their candle- and oil-lamp-lit studios, so that by morning the square of marble or the canvas had been worked to represent a creature not human at all? Were the studios in fact holy places, like temples, where angelic visitors took up positions, letting artists copy them into material form but without wings, pretending that their art represented the human face, the human body?

Cloete accepted that he had never brought classical perfection into existence. He had never managed – not even in his finest surgical work – to remould a face into one of pure beauty, where the balance, in his estimation, between nose, cheekbones, brow and jaw was true and perfect.

Even so, he satisfied the vanities of countless women: those who wished to fill out their lips and those who sought to cut them back; those who wanted to augment their cheekbones; those who felt their noses dominated their faces; those who wished to inhibit the wrinkle-producing muscle movements of the face; those who wanted to laser away superficial layers, vapourizing the signs of age and allowing the skin to regenerate to a new, youthful, deceptive texture.

His waiting room was always full; the great leather sofa and two deep armchairs seated an array of women – and often men – who, displeased with their appearance, were seeking to perfect it. ('In whose terms?' he wanted to ask them. 'By which definition of beauty shall I work and within which parameters?')

As if replying to his unvoiced questions, there were some who brought cut-outs from magazines, and others who named the models he should work from: Julia Roberts for her nose; Angelina Jolie for her lips; Victoria Beckham for her high cheeks; Kerry McGregor for her breasts.

Some patients did not want their identity revealed and arranged consultations in private hours so they did not have to wait publicly. But most sat happily in his waiting room reading magazines, chatting idly about the latest trend in nail colour or dress style. A comparison of his appointment book with Primo's would reveal that they shared many clients.

There was a certain intimacy between the surgeon and his patients. For the patient, in confiding her displeasure in her appearance, her desire to perfect it, her need to look as she thought she was supposed to look, revealed vulnerabilities – both psychological and emotional. Also, particularly where procedures to the body were concerned, she would have to undress. Some women found the atmosphere in Dr Van Rensburg's bright sterile examination room, with its stainless-steel instruments and smell of antiseptic solutions, erotic. He too enjoyed the nudity, the intimacy, and the fact that here was a person yielding completely to his skill, to the work of his hands, to his care, to his precision.

When he took his patient to theatre, when she lay anaesthetized before him, as senseless and vulnerable as a piece of clay, he – masked, gloved and gowned in sterile green cotton – became a god of sorts, an artist-god, who could transform what had been created by another, greater god. Once the surgery was over and enough time had elapsed for healing to take place and bruises to fade, the patient would look in the mirror and behold a better face, a rejuvenated countenance, and be pleased.

At post-operative examinations he would note in the patient's file how well the augmented breasts sat, or how improved was the now taut texture of the facial skin, or how flat the abdomen, now free of the kilos it once carried. Yes, he too would be pleased. But not satisfied. The clay form he had worked upon had been merely enhanced. He had not rendered it into the perfect body or face. His work remained below the benchmark of beauty as he judged beauty to be.

At the end of each day, in his elegantly furnished office, when he wrote his theatre notes, he looked across his desk at the framed reproductions on the opposite wall. Their faces would gaze out from serene and still positions, frozen in time, their beauty captured for ever by their artists: Rossetti's Girl at a Lattice and *Bocca Baciata*; Prinsep's Leonora; Da Vinci's *Testa di fanciulla*; Nimuë in Burne-Jones's *Beguiling of Merlin*.

Sometimes he would take from his drawer a postcard of Michelangelo's sketch of *Testa di Adamo* and study it closely, though he knew well its every detail. Inside himself he ached, so moved was he by the sheer and absolute beauty that the lines depicted.

Cloete's other lover, Sissy Plumb, was the owner of Sissy-and-Esquire, a clothing and body-decor emporium. She too was obsessed with appearance, but appearance of a different sort. She worked with the decoration of the body. She took the body form as it was – fat, thin, ugly, good-looking – and dressed it, robed it, suited it, attired it. She used the skin as a canvas to be tattooed and inscribed with permanent inks. People came to her shop with nothing much in mind, not knowing quite which garment they should wear to weddings, to work, to funerals, to the theatre, to seduce, to rebel, to cope with turning fifty, to heal the heart after a husband's infidelity, to break out of a dull life.

Perched on a high stool at her till, she summed up people as they walked in. Peering at them over her lightly tinted retro diamanté sunglasses, she knew what they needed even before they opened their mouths. It might be a little black leather skirt to be worn without underwear and with a transparent blouse; or a red outline tattooed around the nipples; or a 1920s dress suit worn with an outrageous orange shirt; or a simple cotton shift worn with a string of amber beads and leather sandals. Sissy could read the body's cry for adornment and she furnished this need as no one else in Cape Town could.

At Sissy-and-Esquire, you could buy spectacular clothing (new, seconds and antique) and have your body pierced, bolted, tattooed, scarified or branded. Sissy's emporium stretched from Long Street all the way back to Loop Street; its two storeys and basement housed marvellous clothes and body coverings that she sourced through agents from all over the world.

Two seamstresses and a Malay tailor made up garments for Sissy's own label. She stocked Victorian, Edwardian, retro and sixties clothing, mink coats and fox-pelt stoles – complete with foxes' heads and tails. She sold military jackets (very pricey if they were pre-1900 and bullet-holed), 1920s beaded dance shifts, camel-hair capes from Kashmir, chastity belts, whalebone corsets and burial shrouds. Her stock was seemingly unlimited, its variety outrageous. She even had a selection of flamboyant hats once sported by the Empress Alexandra, last Tsarina of all the Russias, and a little sailor suit (not for sale) said to have been worn by her son, Tsarevitch Alexis, brown-stained by one of his haemophiliac bleeds.

Sissy herself dressed only in white, cream and brown linens. She kept her hair short, spiked and gelled, and smoked through a long holder she claimed once belonged to Alice Keppel, the mistress of King Edward VII. Her fingers were clustered with silver rings, her arms heavy with bracelets.

Sissy's black cat, Esquire, wore a diamanté collar and slept most of the day on the counter, by the till. Her guard and chauffeur, Meduro, a refugee from the Congo, sat on a high stool at the entrance, preventing street children and other undesirables from entering the shop or harassing customers on the pavement. He was a hugely built ebony man who shaved his head and wore a single silver earring in his left ear. His right upper arm bore the deep scar of a machete attack and his back the keloid lines of a lashing. He wore tight denim jeans and military-style boots, with his upper body naked and oiled on hot days.

Sissy rented out two basement rooms to body artists and here they pierced and tattooed clients. Meduro, working in a third basement room, took care of branding and scarification, two new body-art forms. He strapped Sissy's customers down on a surgical bed, heated his irons over a small gas burner and branded them from a choice of some fifty designs, on whichever body part they requested. Because the branding left a smell of burnt flesh, it was done late Saturdays, after the front of the shop had closed. Also, though they considered themselves to be tough macho types (they were generally young neo-Nazi tourists), most of Meduro's clients let out blood-curdling screams as red-hot iron touched flesh. Sissy did not want to disturb other customers.

Scarification was a longer process and each design generally took some months to complete. Most chose to have their patterning done on parts of the body that could be covered: the torso, breast, stomach, back or buttocks. Meduro would cut patterns through the skin, removing the epidermis. He patted pulverized herbs into each incision, to coagulate with blood, then sent the customer home until the scabs hardened. These he later lifted with a surgical hook (a gift from Dr Van Rensburg), allowing the incisions to bleed and repeating the process a number of times until permanent scars were established.

Sissy promoted another form of scarification, one just emerging among the ultra-fashionable – that of designer scars which showed their bearer to have survived a life-threatening attack or accident. These customers she referred to Cloete, who surgically reproduced scars across the jugular, scars that looked as though the throat had been hacked, jagged scars that ran down cheeks and across temples, scars across the wrist to denote suicide survival and even Harry Potter scars to the forehead.

Born in Boksburg, Sissy was the daughter of a used-car salesman who never made good and who drank heavily, beating his wife and abusing his daughters. Sissy knew she was cut out for better things and her artist's eye craved the chance to create adornment and art. She ran away to

Cape Town when she was fifteen. For a number of years she picked up commuting businessmen in hotel lobbies and at the airport, charging a high rate for good quick sex in their hire-cars, parked on Signal Hill overlooking the glittering lights of the city.

She opened a small shop in Long Street when she was not yet twenty, by which time she was already hardened and ruthless. At first she dealt only in second-hand garments and costume jewellery. But with her single-mindedness and good eye for dress, it was not long before her shop had grown into an emporium.

Sissy had been married twice but both marriages ended in acrimony and hatred. She was manipulative and enjoyed the control she wielded over men. She grew bored easily in relationships and made sexual and emotional demands few were prepared to meet.

Now she shared her bed with Meduro and Cloete – though Cloete did not know Meduro slept with her – in the roof apartment above her shop, which was furnished completely in white and cinnamon, and had glass walls and views all round the city. When Cloete called, late at night, Meduro sat motionless on a stool, concealed behind an elaborate Chinese screen, watching their sexual play through the tiny hole an emperor had once used to spy on his concubines.

Sissy enjoyed having sex with Virginia's lover.

Having an affair with the partner of a friend gave her a sense of power. She also liked to have Meduro watching. This heightened her pleasure.

'How is the Contessa tonight, Cloete? Drinking a bit much again?' she asked, arching her eyebrows, one night when he had come straight to her from Virginia. 'I've seen her naked, so I know you've done her breasts. Those scars – was that an error or did you mean them to be so prominent? Is that your signature, Cloete? Is she your work of art?' She lit a cigarette.

'You could say so,' he replied, undressing himself, then taking the cigarette holder from her lips and resting it on an ashtray. 'All my work is my art in some way or another. Like yours is. Don't you feel you are painting when you drape someone with cloth? And isn't there often a little imperfection in your art? Are your seams always straight? Are your choices always right?'

'Always. I make no errors.' She paused, regarding him coolly. 'I want to know whether she chose her breast size. Or did you? They're a bit on the large side, wouldn't you say? She knows what I think about them, so you can be frank with me. She won't mind.' She leant towards him. 'I'm sure you like what you've done for her, but don't you prefer my breasties, my natural little ones? Aren't they better than her pile of silicone?'

Cloete unbuttoned Sissy's dress, took it off, and threw it down at the foot of the bed. He ran a finger across her clavicle, then kissed her neck, cupping a hand over each small breast. He did not answer her probing, but pulled her down onto the bed.

He had worked on her body too. Not her breasts, but her lips, augmenting them so they looked permanently pursed. And he had tidied the lobes of her ears, stretched from heavy earrings. She had wanted him to trim her inner labia so that they remained concealed. 'I don't want to look like I have a red camellia flapping around down there, do I, Cloete?' she had reasoned. But he had refused.

After Cloete left – he never stayed the night – Meduro would pleasure Sissy, for in truth only he could fully satisfy her. 'It's the chiaroscuro, Meduro, that I love,' she once told him. 'My pearl-white skin against your swamp black. And there is still a savage in you. White men are so lame.'

He called her *Maman* and spoke French, the language of his country's colonizers.

Although Sissy Plumb serviced the fashion needs of most of the Long Street community, she was not well liked. She was seductive and predatory and she damaged marriages. As well as knowing how to adorn the body, Sissy also recognized when a body was poorly satisfied sexually. She had a carnal sixth sense and she used it to her advantage, drawing frustrated men to her as a luscious swamp lotus draws night insects. Women were unsettled by her, particularly those who were not good in bed, those who were unimaginative in love, and those who could not stir their husbands' passions because they had no confidence in their bodies.

Two men who were not easy prey were Primo and Pasquale; Primo because he disliked her intensely, and Pasquale because he had already had his time with her and had paid dearly for it. She had long ago ensnared him with her seductive vines and led him through a frenzy of sex on the bar counter of his delicatessen late one night; in the back row of the Labia Theatre while *Bonnie and Clyde* was showing; in De Waal Park when the fountain still worked – at midnight, under its gushing water; and in the men's changing room of the Long Street baths. These sexual encounters soon brought about the end of Beatrice's relationship with Pasquale.

All through their teenage and early adult romance Beatrice had pretended not to be hurt by the many other girls he messed around with. Sissy, however, was someone with whom she knew she could never sexually compete with. Beatrice recognized she would never hold Pasquale as her own. The time had come to let him go.

It was on the day that she decided their relationship was over that Primo, with his marriage proposal in mind, invited Beatrice to meet him in Government Avenue. She thought it was to warn her about something, to caution her about Sissy, for he often gave unsolicited readings into the futures of his friends. But he had something more special in mind. He had come to save her from the unbearable aloneness she had prepared herself to face in giving up Pasquale as her lover.

Beauty, Pasquale told Beatrice, takes many forms. They were upstairs, reclining on the sofa, talking and drinking, on the night before Primo's return.

She lay against him and he played with her hair.

'Is my fruited bread, hot from the oven, its almond-sugar topping turned to copper, not a thing of beauty? And isn't the purple-green of *carciofii alla Veneziana* a splendour to behold?'

'Are you comparing me to an artichoke, Pasqui?' she asked.

'Shall I compare thee to a summer artichoke?' he teased. 'Of course I do, because you have a soft heart. And I compare you to a summer fig, red and ripe. And also to a grilled salmon, trickled with olive oil and touched with sage, because you are delicious. I can't resist you.

'Beatrice,' he said, touching her face. 'Don't go home. Phone Primo when he gets back tomorrow and be straight. Just tell him he's had his twenty years and now it's my turn. We'll all still be friends, only you'll be in my bed and not his.

'And then, make sure you're never alone with him, because he'll enchant you a second time and take you away from me again. You have to be careful when two men love you.'

'Why do two men love me?' she asked coquettishly.

'Because of your thighs which are dimpled and good, like legs of beef; and because of this nice roll you have here in the middle; and your breasts, of course. You have lovely breasts.'

She hit him playfully and they laughed, then grew quiet for a while, for though they were joking, their interlude together was almost at an end, and there was a heaviness between them. Pasquale had already finished off two bottles of wine and now uncorked a third.

'You know, when you left me for Primo, we were still in a relationship. You were my girlfriend, remember? And if you hadn't married him, if you'd married me in the first place, we wouldn't have this mess. Don't you agree there's a mess?'

'Yes, there is. But you started it. You always had a run of other girls, and then your going off with Sissy Plumb just finished everything for me. You hurt me, and you know you did, so don't pretend. At least I only had one other lover. And I married him first.'

'But you agreed to marry Primo without asking me first whether I minded! How could you do that? You told me when you'd already accepted him. You didn't give me a chance. How do you think I felt? Betrayed! That's what I felt. If I'd known you wanted marriage I would have married you immediately and finished with the others. I just had sex with other women. As for Sissy, she's trash, you know that. I was stupid. Immature. I didn't know how to value you. But I loved you.

'At least I would have given you a baby.'

Pasquale got up, filled his glass, and went out to the balcony. He leant over, looking down at the traffic. He turned back to Beatrice. She was crying. 'Don't cry,' he soothed. 'I'm sorry. I'm so sorry. I made the mess, in the past. And now.'

He ran a finger across her lips and kissed them, tasting salt tears. He held her hand, kissing each finger, quiet for a moment, then said, 'Do you remember when we first made friends with Primo? When we saved him from those horrible kids who had cornered him outside my father's store? And he couldn't speak English properly – do you remember? They were pushing him from one to the other. He was crying, remember?'

'Yes.'

'We've been friends so long,' said Pasquale.

'Yes.'

'And now when he finds out, it'll all be over.'

'Yes.'

'Shall I take you back home now? Before he gets in tomorrow? We won't have to say anything. We'll throw away his cards and smash the crystal ball. He'll never know.' He had her face in his hands, trying to make her laugh. 'Don't cry, don't cry Beatrice!'

Unknown to them, Primo was already back. He knew, as he unlocked the door, without even entering their home, that Beatrice was gone. Now he sat at the kitchen table, at the threshold of a new phase of his life, his desert crystals spread across the tablecloth. He sat the whole evening, waiting till morning to make the phone call he knew would end their marriage.

Beatrice spent the first seven years of her life in a bachelor flat in Mill Street, with her unmarried mother, who was secretary to a solicitor in Leeuwen Street, close to the law courts.

Beatrice remembered nothing of the flat except two plastic garden chairs, two mattresses with bedding, a cooler bag and hot-plate. Once there had been a floral carpet and a green-and-beige lounge suite. There had been a coffee table and a glass bowl filled with plastic grapes that seemed so lifelike they made your mouth water for sweetness.

Once there had been a double bed in which a man slept with her mother – a man who smelt musty and sour but also fragrant, and who always had Sen-Sen sweeties in his trouser pockets. He was a man Beatrice never saw during the day, and whom she called Uncle.

There had been a dressing table in her mother's room with a matching set of crystal cosmetic jars and a perfume atomizer. And there had been a painting on the wall, an oil painting in an ornate gilt frame, of the Doge's Palace in Venice, with gondolas in the foreground and angry storm clouds piling up in the sky behind. The colours were a tempestuous mix of reds and darkening blues and deep sea-water greens tinged with orange. Beatrice did not remember the painting itself, but inside of her was a memory of storms. So whenever she saw clouds amassing in the sky, like great galleons preparing for war, blackened and dark and imposing, a sense of familiarity stirred in her.

The same sense of familiarity stirred when certain types of middle-aged men came close to her – men who smelt of cigar smoke and strong after-shave; men whose hair was plastered down to cover a receding hairline; whose skin smelt of alcohol, as though they had drunk so much that their pores were exuding it. This sense of knowing the stranger did not happen often, for this kind of man did not regularly enter Beatrice's life. But on the one or two occasions she had brushed against such a person in the street, or outside the cinema, her hand had automatically gone up to her cheek, as though to protect it from being painfully pinched and twisted. Then a deep and primal rush had come over her to run away, and keep on running.

One day the Uncle had stopped coming to the flat, and her mother had stopped going to work. Instead she sat in the kitchen, smoking cigarettes. One by one everything in the flat was sold and taken away, even the painting and the crystal jars, until Beatrice and her mother were left with just the plastic chairs and nothing else. The Uncle came by once more and took Beatrice and her mother to a boarding house in Long Street. Beatrice never saw him again.

The boarding house was the old Blue Lodge and here her mother slept or wept for weeks on end, until the proprietress, a fat, balding woman called Ruby, told her that the credit the Uncle had left was used up, and she must now work for her accommodation, or leave. So Beatrice's mother (her name was Frankie) began to work as a prostitute, servicing men (mostly sailors) while her daughter played on the pavements with Pasquale and the many children of Long Street's shop owners and merchants.

One day, Frankie asked Pasquale's parents whether they would look after Beatrice for a month while she went to Johannesburg to find her brother. Standing at the counter of their grocery store, she explained that she wanted to make arrangements to leave Cape Town and begin a new, better life. Over the year that she had lived at the Blue Lodge, she had befriended Cornelia and Massimo Benvenuto, and they had grown fond of her, much as they would have been fond of a foundling. Each evening she came down to their shop to buy the same items: two buttered rolls, six slices of salami, a tomato and a tin of soup. Cornelia and Massimo pitied her frailty and lack of confidence, and nurtured feelings of care for her, wondering what had driven so lovely and sensitive a young woman to a life of prostitution. (Each evening Massimo wrapped two slices of fruited bread for mother and daughter to enjoy with their supper, in a room he guessed to be bleak.)

On the day of her departure, Frankie had dressed Beatrice in a yellow frilly party dress, and brought her to the Benvenutos with a small suitcase of clothes. She had kissed her daughter goodbye, left a phone number (which later proved to be wrong) and disappeared, never to be seen or heard of again. When Beatrice had started to cry, Pasquale led her to the back of the shop and gave her his bag of marbles. 'You can keep them till she comes back,' he had said. 'But only if you don't cry.'

Cornelia and Massimo always hoped Frankie would return for Beatrice, so they never handed the child over to the welfare authority, knowing she would inevitably be placed in an orphanage. They never for one moment believed she had intended abandoning her daughter; they thought some misfortune must have befallen her, and that she would come back one day.

Beatrice, too, waited for her mother and, even though she became the third well-loved child in the warm and caring home of Massimo and Cornelia Benvenuto, she never stopped wondering why her mother had not fetched her.

(Years later, an image came up in Primo's crystal ball – but he did not tell Beatrice – of an old

bag-lady standing outside a toyshop, her face pressed
against the glass, weeping:

> *She stands looking in at the shop window from*
> *morning till night;*
> *The porcelain doll inside the shop window has dark*
> *thick hair and rosy cheeks;*
> *The doll wears a dress of yellow lace and ribbons;*
> *The old lady unpacks her trolley;*
> *She lays out cardboard and a blanket; beds down*
> *on the pavement for the night.)*

As children growing up together in Long
Street, Beatrice and Pasquale had a close
and good relationship. Virginia, a rather
prim-and-proper little girl, seldom joined them in
their rough-and-tumble games, preferring to stay indoors while the two of them had fun outside on
the pavement. At first they played with Long Street's
many other children, but once they befriended
Primo they spent their time with him. They became
his only friends.

Primo was an isolated, shy boy, not accustomed to
playing with others. Children found him odd and
teased him because he spoke a strange mix of Italian
and English and often slipped unwittingly into
Latin. This was because his father, in his choice of
literature for his son's reading, ignored the English
classics and concentrated instead on such Roman
poets as Catullus, Tibullus and Ovid. And, of course,

even as a young boy Primo's intuitive and magical powers were evident, and many mothers warned their children to keep away from him, disturbed when he responded to their unvoiced thoughts.

After Beatrice and Pasquale had rescued Primo from the group of taunting children, they brought him into Pasquale's father's grocery store. Massimo Benvenuto took one look at the trembling boy and sat all three children at the table in the back kitchen. Here he served them slices of fruited bread and cups of warm milk, with a drop of Marsala stirred into Primo's. Then, together with Pasquale and Beatrice, Massimo walked the boy home to his father, the watchmaker in Kloof Street.

Massimo was acquainted with the watchmaker and saw him in the synagogue once a year on Yom Kippur, the Day of Atonement. Neither man knew that this was the only time the other attended. Each had his reason for not worshipping regularly.

The watchmaker wanted little to do with God, for God had failed him at his time of greatest need. He addressed God only once a year, and that was to atone for neglecting his ancestral religion. Massimo, by contrast, was not concerned with organized religion and believed that he adequately worshipped God through the way he lived his everyday life. He acknowledged that he had to face God directly for the forgiveness of the past year's sins and short-comings and for this he attended the Yom Kippur services.

Massimo knew no more of the watchmaker than that he was a widower with a young son. So he was surprised when, on striking the knocker, the door was opened by a woman – an attractive woman he had never seen before, one with deeply lovely eyes and silvered raven hair held back in a long plait. She was joined at the door by the watchmaker, Eugenio Verona, who shook Massimo's hand and invited him in. He called out to his son, waiting on the stoep with Beatrice and Pasquale, 'Primo! Welcome your friends inside. Come in and offer them something. *Zia* Lidia has fresh *biscotti*, I'm sure of this.'

Eugenio and Lidia led their unexpected visitors down the length of the passage into the large kitchen. He invited Massimo to sit on the ottoman while Lidia ground freshly roasted coffee beans and filled the espresso machine. She arranged biscuits on a plate and listened shyly as the visitor introduced himself.

Primo took his new friends into his father's workshop, where they stood transfixed as the longcase clocks struck the quarter-hour, not quite in unison, so their chimed announcement took longer than a minute. Then he showed them the treasured bones of time stored in his father's many small drawers – tiny springs and screws and washers and levers and hands and dials. He pulled a suitcase from under the window workbench, saying, 'These are mine. My father just bought them for me at the auction.'

He showed them a clock mounted into the banjo of a small cast-iron negro minstrel. Primo wound it up and, as it ticked, the eyes moved from side to side. He took out two carriage clocks, which he wound up and placed, ticking, on the floor; and a cuckoo clock, which he opened to show the bird's little box and spring and release catch.

Beatrice and Pasquale had never seen such a room. They looked through Primo's kaleidoscope at the tumbling, fragmenting, reforming patterns of colour.

'Can you tell the time?' asked Beatrice.

Primo announced, 'Yes. I can. And I'll teach you. But you must understand that time is just a point of view.'

Lidia brought them biscuits and freshly pressed plum juice, as the clocks all struck again and the three children laughed in delight, knowing they would be friends for ever.

On that long, enchanting afternoon Massimo learnt that Lidia was Eugenio's twin sister ('Though not identical,' she had pointed out). The two men spoke about the Italy they had known as young people, of the war, of their journey out from their war-ruined motherland.

'Our parents were killed by the Fascists, early on in the war,' was all Eugenio disclosed about his family, while Lidia brewed fresh coffee and brought out more biscuits, offering nothing to the conversation.

Massimo explained his visit. He had come about their son, who was a regular customer in his shop. He had noticed, he told them, that the boy was always alone, always shopping and running errands, but never in the company of other children – never playing. 'Should he not be playing with others?' he asked them. 'Going to school? Learning to speak English properly?'

Massimo would relate to his wife, Cornelia, as they lay in bed that night, whispering so as not to wake the three children who shared their room, what a strange and lonely air Lidia had about her, and how beautiful she was.

'She's his sister, Corrie. Fancy none of us knowing the watchmaker has a sister.'

'But who has ever seen her?' asked Cornelia, not giving him time to answer. 'Why does she stay indoors, never come out? What kind of life are they leading? Does she speak English?'

'No, she can't speak English, and, yes, it seems she stays indoors and never goes out,' answered Massimo. 'That's why we always see the boy doing the errands. She has no world but the one inside that strange double house.'

'Poor boy!' said Cornelia. 'What an unnatural life they force on him. Should we try to make friends with them, invite them out for a picnic or a walk along Signal Hill?'

'You must of course invite them, Corrie, but I don't think they'll come. Still, we can help the boy.

Such a nice boy. So good and responsible. With such maturity in those deep eyes. We must get him out of that house more. And what a house! I've never seen so many clocks. Granted, he's a watch-maker. But they're all ringing and striking together. It's enough to drive the sane mad.'

Massimo's visit to the house of 21 and 21A Kloof Street marked a turning point in Primo's life. For a start, he was sent to school, and the English he spoke shed its Latin component and strong Italian accent. Most importantly, his friendship with Pasquale and Beatrice took root.

The careful selection of meats is as important in the making of a good *salame* as is the choice of herbs and spices and the final curing process. Pasquale regularly made three types of salami: *Crespone* (also known as *salame Milanese)*, *salame Genovese* and *salame Napoletano*. For favoured customers he made *finocchiona*, a variation of *salame Fiorentino*, which was flavoured with fennel seeds. The recipes for these salami were regional. The first was particular to Milan, the second to Genoa, the third to Naples, and the *finocchiona* to Florence. That Pasquale was skilled in the making of all four types was exceptional and unheard of outside Italy. He owed this talent to his father, Massimo Benvenuto.

Pasquale's grandfather, Avram Benvenuto, had been a successful and well-respected doctor in Rome during the twenties and thirties. His career and reputation flourished until 1938, when, because he was a Jew, they were cut short by Benito Mussolini's restrictive racial laws. Among other things, these limited his medical practice to serving only Jewish patients, so that his work was severely curtailed. Although Jews in wartime Fascist Italy were at that stage still free from the danger of deportation, daily life became increasingly difficult.

After Mussolini's downfall in July 1943 most Italians celebrated the short-lived tenure of the new prime minister, Pietro Badoglio. Avram Benvenuto, a man of foresight and intelligence, did not. Six German divisions with one hundred thousand soldiers were stationed in Italy during that July. An additional twelve divisions poured into Italy, and in September Germany formally occupied the country, re-establishing Mussolini as its puppet dictator. The arrest and internment of Jews was soon to become government policy. By the time the round-up for deportation began, Avram had already placed his wife and two daughters in a convent, and his son in the safe keeping of his tailor, a veteran who had distinguished himself and been decorated for bravery in both the Libyan War and World War I.

Avram had left his son standing at a prearranged meeting place two blocks from the ancient Roman Theatre of Marcellus. He had watched from a dark alley as the limping figure of the tailor emerged from the shadows, altering his pace so the boy could fall into step beside him. Both walked on and disappeared into the night. The boy carried no case, so as not to arouse suspicion. In his jacket pocket he had a photograph of himself and his family. (Behind them, in the photograph, hung the intricate sixteenth-century tapestry that his father had given the convent where his mother and sisters now hid.)

Avram lingered in the shadows, watching his son walk away, imprinting into his mind, with great care, the image of the boy looking back just once. (It had been impressed upon the child not to wave.) He went back to their apartment for a few nights to close his affairs, and then began to look for a secure and permanent hiding place for himself. He wanted to remain in Rome to be close to his family.

The tailor, a proud old man who had lost a leg to a complicated injury, was disgusted by Mussolini's unequivocal allegiance to Hitler. Two weeks before, his youngest brother, a liberal journalist sympathetic to the plight of the Jews, had been arrested. He had disappeared without trace.

The tailor bricked up the window of a small storeroom adjacent to his workroom at the back of his home and positioned a cupboard in front of its door. It was here that Massimo was to hide, together with the tailor's nephews – two brothers, one a butcher and the other a baker – and a statue of the Virgin Mary.

*   *   *

The butcher and the baker, to avoid being conscripted, had moved from their home town, Sansepolcro, and sought sanctuary with their uncle. The statue had stood in a shrine in the baker's kitchen. She now looked down at them from a corner shelf with a serene smile on her ageless face. The brothers and the statue had been in hiding since 1940, when Italy became Germany's ally in war, and welcomed the young Massimo with care and understanding.

He joined them in their cramped hiding place, where they could not raise their voices and where they spent their time sitting or lying on mattresses, taking turns to walk around the room. Very early each morning, long before dawn, the tailor would push aside the cupboard that sealed their door, and the three would come out of the room to stretch their legs, look at the sky and rinse out their slops bucket.

Whenever they heard the tailor's heavy scissors crash to the ground, they were silent, for this was the tailor's signal that someone was knocking at his front door. In the beginning, each day was marked by the comforting sounds of the tailor's sewing machine. As his work grew scarcer, however, those reassuring sounds ceased.

The tailor did his best to procure food for his concealed family, having assured Avram, 'I will care for your son as though he were my own.' Avram had given him a considerable sum of money,

knowing food would become increasingly expensive
and difficult to buy. Each night the tailor brought
in a pail of fresh water, a loaf of bread, fresh beets
and herbs, boiled potatoes, perhaps an onion. Occasionally there would be eggs. Once he managed
to bring a great luxury: a wild hare, roasted slowly
with garlic and rosemary.

To help cope with their confinement and pass the
time, the butcher and the baker began to describe
the preparation of their culinary specialities. They
started on the day when the boy was in despair
and crying softly, for he had imagined that his
father would visit, but now knew that this was not
possible.

uppose,' said the butcher, winking at his
brother, 'that I were to take a half-kilo of
donkey meat and a half-kilo of horse but
could find no other meat because our esteemed
leader *Il Duce* had eaten it all himself. Would I
be able to make a *salame* good enough for King
Victor Emmanuel to enjoy? And what if I had garlic
but no cardamom? Or what if the peppercorns had
been confiscated by a heartless Fascist? What
could I prepare to place on the royal table? Could I
make a true *salame*? Or could I make up only a
sausage without taste, a sausage moist and flaccid,
a sausage fit only for Nazi palates?

'Come, boy, sit up, don't lie there in sorrow! These
are important questions I raise. I want your opinion!

Imagine I have a kitchen. Better still, imagine this room we call home is a kitchen equipped with chopping boards and knives and a larder and graters and pots and steaming cauldrons. So come inside it and help me sort through my recipes. Stop your weeping now! We must solve this problem before the war ends and the last Nazi has mended his foolish ways, for after that we will have food aplenty and no time to discuss the basics of a good *salame*.'

'And imagine,' said the baker, taking his brother's cue and looking up at his statue of Mary, 'that we must bake a fruited bread for the Christmas table of the Holy Virgin, but we have no crystallized fruit, no sugar, not a drop of sweet wine. What if the flour were black? Could we bake her a cake so sweet that she would come down from heaven to our wartime Italy to fetch it?'

'No, it will not be possible. The salami will have no taste and the fruited bread will be bland. Neither will be fit for King or Virgin,' continued the butcher. 'We must fetch the ingredients we require and do the job properly. Come, boy! We are going on a journey or two. We are going to ride camels and mules across Asia. We are going to take a ship from Naples and sail the high seas from there to Africa because we must buy, from merchants in faraway lands, the choicest spices and herbs and preserved fruits to make the best salami and fruited bread since Adam followed Eva out of Paradise!'

103

So the butcher and the baker took Massimo on a long imaginary journey, first following Marco Polo's route from Venice through Asia Minor to collect ingredients for the salami and fruited breads they wanted to make. The journey had its hazards: the butcher described bandits and lepers in the hills, and the baker told of snakes and scorpions among the desert rocks where they slept. They came upon almost impassable canyons and flooded rivers; they had to eat the flesh of serpents baked in the hot sun; they lost their way in the Gobi desert; they escaped galloping hordes of Mongols and survived fevers and deliriums.

The butcher and the baker outlined a second provisioning journey, in which they raised the sails of a great ship and set off, leaving behind the Mediterranean, crossing the Atlantic ocean almost as far as Brazil, then catching the winds that carried their vessel down to the edge of Africa. From there they beat their way up the east coast until the trade winds filled their sails, taking them to the spice islands of Pemba, Mafia and Zanzibar, then on to India. On this journey they bought sacks of cloves, vanilla, cardamom, nutmeg, mace and ginger.

But this was not all they needed, so they had to travel again. On a third journey they sailed to the Americas to bring back the finest sugars and stone-ground flours. All these they stored in an imaginary dark and cool cellar under the tailor's house.

'The best place to buy meat will be the markets

of north Africa,' announced the butcher. 'For there the livestock grazes on exotic grasses so the meat is succulent, like pummelled veal. The milk is not good, it is too pungent, but the meat has the wonderful taste of the earth. We must sail across the Mediterranean again. This time, I think we will take a Phoenician sailing vessel to Alexandria. We will be guided by the beam of a great lighthouse and we will consult Nubian herbalists, not Egyptians, on how best to cure meat, for we do not want our salami to taste of saltpetre, do we?' he asked, hugging the boy, who was cradled in his arms.

Outside in the real world, grown men at war were laying waste Europe. But in his hiding place Massimo, who had lost all sense of time and reality, was learning to cook. He and his fellow fugitives put on imaginary white aprons, sharpened their knives and began to process and cure a variety of salami.

'Of course, *salame* is not *salame* without pork. You Jews must relax a bit with those antiquated rules the rabbi gives you,' the butcher argued. 'We need the succulent meat of piglets fed only on oats and cream.'

'Leave your provocative talk about pork!' the baker responded. 'And before the war is done, find a way to make salami without pork for our Jewish boy, one so delicious that it will seem that a pig fed entirely on milk and honey was sacrificed in the making.'

105

'And what might you know about meat, dear brother?' asked the butcher, in mock argument. 'You with your lily-white pastry hands. Don't talk to me about pigs and pork and I won't talk to you about sugars and flour. Stay in your cake department.'

And so throughout their confinement they travelled the world, collected ingredients, argued their way through countless recipes and worked hard in their kitchen until they had prepared a good variety of Italian salami. So involved in their fantasy did they become that they could virtually taste their abstract meats and, with their eyes closed, identify them:

'*Fiorentino!* With fennel. *Mamma mia!* I will die it is so delicious.'

'*Crespone!* Oh God in Heaven, yes! Yes! Aha! And with whole peppercorns.'

'*Napoletano!* I am speechless. It is more than perfect.'

'*Genovese! Santa Maria!* I can taste the pork. Is there pork in Paradise?'

When their cellar was finally hung full with salami, it was time to turn their attention to the fruited bread, for the baker had made a vow to the Virgin Mary that, before the war ended, they would have for her an offering of the best fruited bread in Italy. In the meanwhile, Massimo had developed a special relationship with her. Every night, in the dark, while the butcher and baker slept, the statue came to life and she stepped down from her plinth, assuming human proportions. In the glow of her halo she lay with Massimo, as his mother used to, holding his head in her arms and singing Hebrew lullabies. The Virgin Mary let him play with the ruby-red beads of her rosary, as his mother had let him play with her jewelled necklace.

When he awoke each morning she would be back on her shelf, smiling down at him.

It was now the baker's turn to take the lead. The fruited bread must have fragrance, texture and a taste that did not overwhelm but which was discreet and demure. It must be light and airy but not vacuous. The yeast must not leave a heavy taste. The delicate flavours of vanilla and cinnamon should be well balanced with those of ginger, nutmeg and mace, for too much of one spice could overpower another and ruin a fruited bread.

Sometimes they would bake as many as six breads a day in their quest for the perfect loaf. In the evenings, they would taste and discuss each one. These were always good, but not good enough. Sometimes it was a gingerbread that came out of the oven, sometimes fig bread. Once, as they were still working out the quantities of orange and lemon peel, the bread was slightly tart and deemed a failure.

It so happened that a perfect fruited bread came out of the oven on the very morning that the tailor, tears streaming down his wrinkled face, moved the cupboard aside to announce, with a bottle of wine in hand, that war had ended. A few weeks earlier, Mussolini had been executed by Communist partisans.

The four stood silently for a moment but soon became raucous as they embraced and laughed and shouted for joy.

'Wait! Wait! One moment, please!' demanded the baker, his hands in the air to stop his friends from leaving the room. 'Before we rush out to the free world, we must first complete something. We are not yet finished in here. I must open the oven.'

Massimo, the butcher and the tailor stood to attention while the baker, humming softly, lifted from the imaginary oven the finest fruited bread ever made. First he sprinkled it with finely powdered almonds and sugar soaked in a rare Macedonian wine, then he raised it in the air and, with his eyes closed, announced, 'Holy Virgin, *Regina Mundi*, accept this our humble offering in thanks for our safekeeping and the liberation of Italy.'

He placed the fragrant bread, rich with crystallized kumquat, red fig, ginger and the zest of mandarin, onto an imaginary altar in the centre of the room and bowed his head, for he knew the mother of God was smiling down from heaven at this little miracle.

The tailor, limping on his ill-fitting prosthesis, led his nephews and Massimo out of their hidden room, through his modest home and into the Italian sunlight. No one spoke until the butcher turned to Massimo and shook his hand. 'Young Massimo,' he said, 'these are not tears in my eyes. I am not crying. It is only that my eyes are not accustomed to the brightness. You were brave through our ordeal and I would like you to take my salami recipes into your future and make your fortune with them.'

The baker placed his hands on Massimo's shoulders, saying, 'Nor do I cry; mine are tears from heaven. Forget our captivity and remember only our freedom. The fruited bread is the miracle of life. Hand it on to your children. And be wise, do not circumcise your Jewish sons. Hide their lives behind their harmless little foreskins in case this anti-Semitic madness ever sweeps the world again.

'As for us, we commissioned the making of a sailing vessel, in the very month those ill-bred Nazis arrived. We will now fetch it from a secret shipping yard near Naples, for it is sure to be ready and waiting.'

'Yes,' said the butcher, taking over from his brother. 'We will sail away to the east, for silks, and only hope that pirates in the South China Sea do not apprehend us.'

'Nor pirates in the Bay of Bengal,' interrupted the baker. 'We will fetch you when you are a grown man, when you have completed your studies and found your bride. We will clothe her in silks and fineries, and we will prepare the wedding feast ourselves. I alone will bake the cake. Twelve tiers, it will have, each one different, and the whole coated in rose-fragranced cream and cherries.'

'But before we sail,' said the butcher, 'we will go home, back to our home town, to look again upon the greatest picture in the world – Piero della Francesca's fresco of the Resurrection of Christ – to pay homage before it, for we too have been resurrected from a tomb, and we too walk out alive again and redeemed from war.'

'Now stop your weeping, boy,' soothed the baker. 'Your father will be here to fetch you, this very afternoon, I'm sure of it. Think of the reunion with your mother and sisters. Think of the feasting and celebrations. Think of the space you will have – you'll be able to run and play again. Those thin little legs will fill out. You will have colour in your cheeks.

'Until we meet again, may the Holy Virgin protect your coming and your going. Now goodbye.'

The brothers collected their few belongings from inside, then embraced the young Massimo and their uncle, and set off for the station with the statue of the Virgin Mary and a shared case, each wearing a new suit that their uncle had made in anticipation of a free Italy.

But things were in turmoil. The trains were not running. While deciding what to do and how to get back home, they were apprehended by a deranged soldier who shot them behind the station, maliciously and without ceremony, accusing them of being deserters and thieves. (Who in war-torn Italy can buy a new suit? he had wanted to know). A stray bullet cut across the Virgin's forgiving face.

assimo waited for his father to fetch him but was soon to learn that neither his parents nor his sisters had survived the war. The old tailor, unable to trace any living relative, kept him on as his own son, sewing him a new suit of clothes every year – until arthritis crippled his hands – and imbuing him with a sense of good dress and demeanour.

'Massimo,' he would mumble through lips holding pins as he measured cloth. 'At night, a man wears pyjamas. And during the day, in his *orto*, while he digs potatoes and feeds the chickens, he wears an overall. But otherwise, he wears a suit. A man always wears a good suit.'

'And Massimo,' he would call out as he cut cloth, 'when you marry, your wife must not work outside of the home. You must make enough money to keep your wife well. Women must be loved and cared for.'

'Massimo,' he would point out as they sat on the bench outside their front door, 'do you see that woman there, across the road? She has been trying for many years to marry me. Ever since my Enrica died, she has come to me at the market, every market day, and asked if I am tired of living alone. I do not live alone now, I tell her. I have a son.

'So come, my young son. Why are you so quiet all the time? What can you tell me that I need to know about life?'

The boy had little to say, for his thoughts were always out to sea, braving wind and waves, enduring calms, hauling in nets of silver barracuda, watching the Southern Cross slip down into the ocean as the earth turned; or riding mules across endless red landscapes, gathering wild honey, looking out for vagabonds and all the while laughing with his two friends, the butcher and the baker.

When Massimo reached his twenty-first birthday, he decided to travel, hoping to come across his friends somewhere on the high seas. By then the tailor was in the care of nuns, for he had grown feeble and forgetful. He passed his days dozing in an invalid chair, under the cypress trees of their convent garden, dreaming of military manoeuvres in the hot Libyan desert.

Under a bright blue sky Massimo said his sad farewell. Black swallows circled overhead, and church bells celebrated the *Festa del Sacro Cuore*.

The tailor, in the twilight of memory, thought that Massimo was setting off to war in the African desert. 'Mind,' the old man cautioned, lifting a warning arthritic finger. 'Do not drink water from wells, for the enemy pours poison into them. And if they capture you, be sure to slit your own throat, for they are bastards of cruelty. They will tie you upside down to a palm and leave you to dry out slowly in the sun, while hawks pick at your eyes.

'And, my son, if you come across a mound marked by a small wooden cross on which is scratched G. B. 1911, will you greet Giacomo Brescascin, my Captain. Tell him I have fresh water for his men.'

A nun stepped forward and whispered to Massimo that it was time for him to leave. The old man was crying, calling out for help, for he could see in the distance a convoy of lost ragged soldiers dragging a wounded comrade, battling to find their way through desolate desert terrain.

Massimo took a train to the docks of Naples, where he was surprised to find not a single sailing ship or Phoenician boat destined for the Far East. Disappointed, he bought a one-way ticket for passage on a British vessel bound for Cape Town. He had with him a leather pouch containing his mother's ruby necklace. His father had left it in safe keeping with the tailor. He also had the money his father had paid for his son's maintenance. The tailor had not spent a single lira of it.

assimo arrived in Cape Town speaking the rudimentary English he had learnt from the galley hands on board ship. He had found his way down to the kitchen, drawn by the dull smells of boiled potatoes and grilled meat, to investigate the culinary sacrilege being committed there. During the six weeks of passage, so as not to be idle, he washed dishes and harnessed all the English he could. He tried to teach the ship's cook the secrets he had been given, but the cook was an unwilling pupil. He had always boiled cabbage and carrots and had never used herbs and spices. Why should he now change?

'Salt and pepper! Is quite good enough!' he shouted in staccato sentences. 'Garlic! Makes breath stink! Women, they not kiss stinky mouth!'

With a cigarette clamped between his lips, ash dusting his work surface, his great arms flaunting tattoos of anchors and eagles, he rolled out pastry and wrapped it around sausage meat. 'Sausage roll!' he shouted. 'Very good! Very easy!'

In Cape Town Massimo took a room at the Flamingo Hof in Kloof Street. Each morning he was served what was described as an English breakfast. This comprised two fried eggs, fried tomato, sweetcorn, baked beans, two fatty bacon rashers and a sausage served on a greasy white plate embossed with a Union Castle logo. Toast stacked in a pewter rack, little rounds of butter, marmalade and a pot of strong black coffee completed the meal.

Every morning Massimo sat alone at a table covered with a starched white tablecloth, listening to and absorbing the English spoken all around him. A set of heavy cutlery, also once belonging to Union Castle Lines, flanked his plate. At the surrounding tables sat uniformed men, clerks and secretaries who ate hastily and then rushed off to their jobs.

He had nowhere to go. Also, his period of confinement had distorted his sense of time, so he never hurried and would spend an hour, if not longer, at breakfast in the gloomy dining room of the Flamingo Hof. He would reflect upon the English breakfast before him, which he never ate. It had been fried the night before and heated through for the morning meal. The oil used was not the finest, nor the freshest. The tasteless sausage had the texture of cardboard and would never be suitable for the table of King or Virgin.

One morning a heavily built man wearing khaki shorts and big boots strode over to Massimo and, showing off to the ladies in the dining room, asked in mock Italian-English, as he lit a cigarette and picked a fleck of tobacco off his tongue, 'Whya yoo nevah eata tha food? The food no gooda eenuf fora yoo? Yoo wanna tha macaroni? *Si! Si!*'

The ladies all sniggered behind their serviettes. Holding the stage he continued, 'Yoo wanna your *mamma* cooka yoo tha spuugetti?'

Massimo, aware he was the butt of a joke and not knowing how to respond, looked down at his greasy breakfast. Though most mornings the sight of oily eggs did not bother him, this morning he felt the nausea rise up. He slapped his serviette to his mouth as the retching seized him, pushed his chair out from under himself and ran from the dining room, laughter bursting out behind him. To his absolute shame, he threw up in the hall. Amid the hilarity, the man's voice boomed, 'For Cris' sake! The little wop's hurled his gut!'

Massimo could not stay at the Flamingo Hof a moment longer. As he packed his suitcase he finally faced the fact that he had no one in the world to call his own. His parents and sisters were dead and his beloved surrogate father was senile. There was no way of locating the butcher or the baker – he reasoned they were probably on the high seas somewhere, or trekking across the Himalayas in search of yak butter. As he reflected upon the cold hard race of people he now found himself amongst – in the five weeks he had been in residence not one person had greeted him – there came a tap at his bedroom door. He opened it hesitantly. There stood a young woman.

'I just want you to know,' she began, 'I did not laugh at you. And I think the man was very rude. And I'm so sorry for what happened, I don't want to stay another moment in this hotel. That's all I want to say.'

Massimo could not concentrate – he was too upset – so he could not grasp the meaning of her English words. He understood her to say that his behavior was no laughing matter; that he was a rude man; that she was sorry he had behaved so improperly in the dining room; and that he should leave the hotel.

He wanted to apologize, but all the English he knew evaporated in the heat of his embarrassment.

The only words he could summon were 'salt and pepper', but he had enough sense not to respond with these. He just sighed, pointed to his suitcase to show that he was already on his way, and sat dejectedly on his bed. He looked so sad, in the dingy bedroom of the Flamingo Hof which had nothing of comfort in it, that the young woman sat next to him and put her arm around him, for he had started to cry and she had never seen a grown man cry.

Massimo settled into her embrace as though he had always known her. Cornelia Boshof was her name, she told him, taking a hanky from her bag, and she had come to Cape Town from the Boland to look for work.

They checked out together and walked the short way to Long Street, she a willowy girl wearing a simple cotton frock, her long blonde wavy hair tied back from her face; he a tall slender upright young man carrying both their cases. They booked into the old Phoenix Hotel, where the breakfasts were also greasy, and where they slept in separate beds until they married some six months later.

Each morning they drank their coffee on the upstairs veranda. Leaning over the ornate Victorian balustrade, watching traffic flow by down below, Massimo wondered how he could earn a living good enough to keep his wife and still be able to afford two new suits each year.

'Corrie,' he announced one day, pointing across the road at a derelict building which had its windows and door boarded up. 'You see the building? You see the building there? I am to open a grocery shop. I am to make salami and fruited bread to sell. That is how I will make our money, Corrie. That is how we will live.'

After much deliberation, and against Cornelia's advice, Massimo decided to pawn his mother's ruby necklace. He took it from its pouch and held it to the light. The blood colour of its nine jewels made his heart ache. 'My mother, she will understand, Corrie. And I only give it for pawning. I do not sell it.'

In Solomon's Pawn Shop he looked down through the glass counter at the lockets, bracelets, signet rings, fob watches, strands of pearls, gold chains, cameos and mourning brooches that others, in positions similar to his, had pawned. A deep sadness seized him. The necklace had been his grandmother's and she had given it to his mother on her wedding day. He closed his eyes and remembered them against his mother's neck, remembered stretching up as a child to touch them when she leant down to kiss him. He remembered learning to count to ten with the aid of the jewels. 'Nine rubies and your mamma's heart makes ten,' his mother's voice rang out now from memory.

'Is there something I can do for you, sir?' asked Emanuel Solomon, behind the counter. 'Are you wanting to buy something?'

His voice brought Massimo back from his reverie. 'No, not to buy. I come to pawn. I come to pawn the rubies of my mother.' He took the necklace from his inner jacket pocket and placed it into Mr Solomon's outstretched hand, saying, 'I am to rent the empty shop on this road and I am to open a grocery store. For this, I must have cash.'

Emanuel Solomon gave a hard look at the man with the rubies who spoke English laden with a strong Italian accent, whose eyes were tear-filled and who every now and then wiped his nose on a white handkerchief. Mr Solomon recognized all the tell-tale signs – for he saw them often in his profession – of a young man breaking his heart as he sold (for pawning was really selling) his mother's jewels, or his father's watch or his grandfather's gold sovereign, just to have some necessary ready cash.

He estimated each oval jewel's weight: the central ruby at a carat and a half and the other eight graduating from one carat to a half-carat each. With a loupe and under the strong light of his lamp, he checked for the growth lines within each jewel to confirm they were genuine. He judged that the exquisite necklace was of French craftsmanship and dated it mid-eighteenth century. Assessing a value, he made his offer.

'I sell my mother!' Massimo suddenly cried.

'Yes, indeed,' said Emanuel Solomon. 'You'll be sorry to lose this. And lose it you will. For collectors come here and buy what they recognize as unique. This is an extraordinary piece. Let me suggest something; I'll pawn it for you, but I won't place it here, on view; I will keep it in my safe, as a deposit against a loan adequate to set up your shop. When you pay back the loan, with interest, I'll return the necklace.'

Massimo, overcome by the stranger's offer, struggled to express his gratitude, and managed only a hearty speechless handshake. There was silence as each man stood looking at the other; the older one remarking to himself how vulnerable the younger looked, how strangely innocent, like a boy who had grown up away from the world. And Massimo was silent because of the prayer he was reciting within himself, that God grant this Emanuel Solomon, and all his sons and daughters, and all the generations which followed them, until the end of time, prosperity and health.

In their Phoenix Hotel room that night he recounted to Cornelia how Emanuel Solomon had wrapped the necklace in tissue paper, then sealed it in a buff envelope and locked it in his safe. He had filled out a loan form, which they both signed, and shaken Massimo's hand.

'I am to bake a fruited bread for him, Corrie. The first fruited bread in the city will be for our new friend, Emanuel Solomon.'

Massimo took his wife's hands and kissed them both, then led her to the balcony, where they sat, looking across at the shop, and made plans. They would live upstairs, above the store, as did all the other Long Street shopkeepers and their families. On the balcony they would grow potted lemon trees and palms. In the back courtyard they would nurture herbs and vegetables and climbing roses. They would cherish every moment of their life together, and take nothing for granted.

*M*assimo opened his grocery store, Da Massimo, on a rising moon, because the baker had once cautioned him never to begin a new enterprise on a waning moon, or it would surely fail. He stocked it with imported pastas, tomato conserve, olive oils, balsamic vinegars, and coffees, making a living good enough to repay his debt to Emanuel Solomon and retrieve his mother's ruby necklace. In time he was able to buy the shop and refurbish it. For this was another thing he had learnt during his confinement, that to pay a landlord was like pouring water into a cracked jug. 'For what to enrich a landlord?' he remembered the baker asking.

Ever mindful of Emanuel's kindness, he baked him a fruited *challah* every Rosh Hashana, round as tradition required it, to herald a good year ahead.

Though Massimo excelled as a grocer, he never managed to establish himself as a salami maker and baker of fruited breads, for in those early years only the small Italian, Portuguese and Greek communities had any appreciation of these specialities. Not even his fruited bread made inroads onto the tea trays of the English and Afrikaaners, who remained loyal to their sponge cakes and scones, *koeksisters* and *boerebeskuit*. ('Leave little mouthfuls out to tempt them. And if it takes a century to change their tastes, let it take a century,' the butcher advised him in a dream one night.) So Massimo left slices of salami and fruited bread in bowls on his counter for customers to savour and enjoy, though it would be his son and not he who conquered the conservative English and Afrikaans palates.

Massimo and Cornelia had two children, both born at home, above their shop, delivered by Simeon Baldinger, the apothecary and father of Dr Adam Baldinger. Massimo named their son Pasquale, after the butcher, and, following the baker's cautioning, did not circumcise him. He named his daughter Virginia, in honour of the Virgin Mary, to whom the baker, Leonardo, had dedicated his work. Throughout his life Massimo heeded the tailor's advice by never letting his wife go out to work, and he always wore a suit, however hot the weather.

Each Easter and Christmas, he sent cards to his two friends. Never sure where they might be, he posted several at one time, *poste restante*, to Cairo, Istanbul, Zanzibar, Bombay, Peking and Madeira. He also sent cards to the tailor, even though he was senile. The nuns would tell the old man they were cards from his son, in Africa, and he would weep, for Africa meant only three things to him: desert sands, thirst and death.

irginia had shown no interest in the kitchen – her talents, when she was young, lay with the visual and fine arts – but the young Pasquale absorbed their father's culinary litany with wonder. As he grew up he helped in the grocery shop after school, serving at the counter and stacking shelves. All the while he listened to his father's fantastic stories of journeys and provisioning. His father taught him to cook, and even as a young lad Pasquale could prepare food that brought songs to the lips of the coarsest man and lightened the dullest heart. More than this, his father also taught him where to source such rarities as hundred-year-old Chinese cherries preserved in juniper liqueur.

Long before Italian cuisine became fashionable, Pasquale renamed and transformed his father's modest grocery shop into Da Pasquale. It was destined to become the most popular delicatessen and bar of the day. Right from the start there was something different, something special, something distinctive about the food he served. He never kept to a set menu, instead deciding at the start of each day what he would serve. His decisions rested on which fruits and vegetables were seasonally available at the markets, or what he fancied eating himself. No one local was foolish enough to order anything so mundane as a mixed grill or hamburger. When unsuspecting tourists ventured in, wanting a pork pie and chips, or a hot dog, Lovemore or Dambudzo would gently usher them out and direct them towards the city centre. And woe betide anyone provocative enough to ask for commercial ketchups and mayonnaises – these pollutants never crossed the threshold to disgrace the Da Pasquale tables.

His mood influenced his cooking. A *ragù* prepared in a fit of pique or passion would not have quite the taste of one cooked during a time of melancholy. Unlike a Woolworths meal, which could be relied upon to have the same colour, texture and taste every time one bought it, each meal from Da Pasquale had a singularity about it. It bore the signature of Pasquale's temperament.

His temperament had been wild at times, for his experiences as a young soldier in the Angolan war had left him brutally stripped of his mental equilibrium. He was medically discharged before completing his military service and later suffered a series of breakdowns. There were times, as a young man, when flashbacks tore him from the present and threw him into flaming villages; garbed him again in the camouflage of a soldier swinging his automatic rifle from right to left and right again, mowing down children and women and old men.

Massimo tried to hold him when such ravings

seized his son, but Pasquale would throw his father off, raging, his mouth twisted, his teeth bared, his arms in spasm. Cornelia would run down to call the newly qualified Dr Adam Baldinger and send Virginia to fetch Primo. Primo would hold his friend down while Dr Baldinger injected him with sedative. Pasquale would be hospitalized until the nightmare of war retreated once more into the shadows.

assimo and Cornelia aged with grace and dignity, living with Virginia in the back ground-floor apartment of her brothel. It had a small courtyard with a fountain where Massimo still tended potted lemon trees and palms. Cornelia spent her time knitting jumpers for her family, for Beatrice and Primo, and for Virginia's ladies.

On the midwinter morning of Massimo's seventieth birthday his memory cast up before him the painting of the Resurrection which the butcher and baker had described and which, though he had never actually seen it, he could now identify.

He lay in bed, in the winter-dark before daybreak, and stared in amazement at the resurrected Christ through a dream space that was neither waking nor sleeping. He could hear his friends' voices, clear and strong in the background, as they said goodbye to the youth he once was. 'When we have finished our journeying, and you are a grown man, we will meet together in our home town, Sansepolcro, at Piero della Francesca's fresco. Come with your betrothed to where the Roman soldiers sleep with the Christ figure standing behind them, tall and triumphant over death. You will find your way to the fresco without difficulty. Ask anyone for direction to the Law Courts. We will be waiting on the steps for you.'

Massimo tried to hold onto the dream, to stay in that place of mirage, but could not. Cornelia was up. She had opened the shutters to let in the winter light. Virginia had brought them their coffee. The image of the painting had dissipated into day.

He dressed solemnly and, as soon as the shops opened, made his way to Clarke's Bookshop to ask if there was a book on Piero della Francesca.

The bookseller showed him a framed print of *The Resurrection* hanging on the wall. 'The most beautiful painting in the world,' his friends had said of it. The young woman told how the first owner of the bookshop, Anthony Clarke, as an Allied gunner officer during World War II, had held back from shelling the town, where there were thought to be German soldiers, because he knew of the fresco and did not want to destroy it.

Massimo stood before the framed picture for a long while, holding his hat in both hands against his chest. Yes, he thought. It is as my friends described it: the sleeping Roman soldiers – how could they sleep with so imposing a figure rising from the dead behind them? Yes, the pained face of the risen

Christ contrasted with his strong beautiful body. Yes, the sarcophagus with its straight lines. Yes, the sinuous cylinders of the tree trunks in the background – those on the left bared by winter, and those on the right heavy with leaves.

'Has this picture always hung here?' he asked.

'No,' replied the bookseller. 'I went to Sansepolcro last year, to see the original. I bought this print there.' She stood next to him, contemplating it. 'The fresco could have been destroyed by just one shell. But it wasn't.'

'Where is Mr Clarke?' asked Massimo.

'He's no longer alive. But he's well honoured for having saved the fresco. There is a street named after him in Sansepolcro – Via Anthony Clarke.'

Massimo thanked her and walked out, the world hazed by his tears.

A few days later, he woke early and, with an intent look in his eye, dressed hurriedly and, calling for Cornelia to follow, set off down Long Street, heading for the sea. Alarmed at his uncharacteristic behaviour, she went after him, imploring him to come back home. Anyone leaning over his balcony that early morning would have seen an elderly man wearing a suit, his white shirt unbuttoned, his black jacket and tie flapping behind him, a hat perched on his white hair and a singular expression on his face, striding, somewhat shakily, ahead of his wife. The onlooker would have noted that the old lady wore slippers, and a dress so hurriedly put on that it was inside out. They would have marvelled at her long grey hair, loosened from its usual coil, and the ease with which she kept up her husband's fast pace.

Massimo led the way down to the docks and out to the end of the breakwater. Here he stood, waiting for a vessel to come over the horizon, a great merchant ship in full sail, bearing a cargo of pepper, vanilla pods, nutmeg and mace, and, smuggled in its hold, bales of cashmere and pure Chinese silk. He had an appointment to keep with his old friends, the butcher and the baker. When they had bid him farewell, so many years ago, he had promised to meet them, when he would be a grown man, with a beautiful lady at his side. The day had come. He was ready. It was time to catch a ride on their great sailing vessel, and sail back home to Italy – he and his bride reunited with his two best friends.

While Pasquale, Virginia and Beatrice and all their friends frantically searched the streets and parks of Cape Town, Massimo stood on the end of the breakwater for the whole day and night, in a roaring northwest wind, with Cornelia at his side.

Primo found their bodies, visioned in his crystal ball:

> *Grey mist rolls in from the sea, now covering them;*
> *Then lifting and moving back to the ocean;*
> *They lie snuggled together, the old lady wearing*
>   *her husband's jacket;*

128

The old man's hat blown away by the wind and
caught against a dolos.

The forces of both good and malevolence, once set on a trajectory in the form of a spell or incantation, are not easily recalled. Until Beatrice left him, Primo had restricted his services to soothsaying and harmonious magic. When people had asked him to cast spells that harmed their partners and spouses, he declined. He had always refused to enchant and influence reluctant lovers on behalf of rejected and spurned suitors. He would not bewitch. He had never helped his friends manoeuvre their way out of difficult poker hands.

So he had no experience of malicious or manipulative magic. His shoelace spell had been cast only to irritate, not to cause harm, and Primo delighted in the harassment it would cause. But the spells set to spoil Pasquale's fruited breads and salami were by their nature in the realm of evil, and, even though Primo believed he had, as he said to himself, put them on hold, the truth is he had not adequately harnessed them. He did not know that they had taken their course and would indeed reach their targets.

After Beatrice had been gone nearly six weeks, with no sign of returning, Primo, his heart riven by loneliness, again tried his hand at intrusive magic, asking aloud: Why have you not phoned? Can you leave and simply forget me? Where has our good past gone? Can it just evaporate to nothing, become mere shimmering, be reduced to this, to your leaving me with no word of farewell, with no understanding of my broken heart?

Standing under the mulberry tree, he prepared a spell to influence her aura, her energy field, so that she would suddenly think of him and come home. Then he would ask her to forgive whatever wrong he had done, and come back to him, for his life had no meaning without her. He reached out and picked a few of the berries, and pressed them between his fingers, then threw them down. Absentmindedly he ran his hand across his forehead, staining it a purple-red, so it looked as though he had been struck across the head by a sword, and now bore a deep and bleeding gash.

Primo wondered: Do you lie with him in his arms, in his bed? Yes, there is no second bed in his room, and there is no second room. Do I come to mind when he holds you? Or does he have you now as his own? Could I have loved you better when you were with me? Yet I love you so well. No woman has turned my head, or my thoughts, or my heart. Only you. No other woman has known my body. But I have failed you, it seems. How did he lure you? Has he always been there, lying in wait, pretending to be my brother, waiting for me to be away, ready to take you from me? Primo could have looked into his crystal ball for answers, but he did not.

Even though the spell Primo prepared was not

a complex one, he misaligned certain of its co-
ordinates and invoked not the return of Beatrice, but
the arrival of the Devil.

The Devil did not arrive in any spectacular
fashion. His presence was unannounced and
he came without fanfare. Primo barely noticed
him as he stood on the stoep of 21A, waiting.

Primo had just returned from the shops and
was fumbling for keys when he became aware of a
presence at his side. He turned to face the person,
about to explain that he had retired from his profession and could be of no help, when he intuited
that this was no mere mortal, but a supernatural
visitor. Though surprised, he unlocked the door and
motioned to the Devil to enter, then led him down the
length of the hall to the kitchen.

The Devil looked around at the disorder and
mess, his eyes settling on the withered violets.
'Why did you call me?' he asked Primo, his amber-
brown eyes penetrating but kind. 'What is it that you
want?'

'I haven't called anyone. I'm a recluse. Who are
you?' asked Primo.

'I am the archangel Lucifer, Guardian of Hell. The
Angel of Dresden.'

The visitor was not wearing a red cloak, nor did
he have horns and tail. His face was not blighted
with pockmarks, nor was his breath foul. In fact,
contrary to all religious imagery, he looked just like

an angel, robed and winged, with thick shoulder-length mahogany curls. He was tall, as tall as Primo, and, like Primo, strongly built with powerful shoulders and a broad back. His robe was woven of the finest cream-coloured linen and had two openings on the back through which his wings – splendours in rose-crimson and gold – emerged. An embroiderer might have observed that the edges of these openings were decorated in herringbone stitch; that the yoke was worked in two-sided Italian cross-stitch, whipped-run and tambour, all in fine gold thread; and that the edges of his wrist-length sleeves were finished off in griffon Assisi work. On his feet, the Devil wore embossed kid-leather shoes. About him lingered the soft fragrance of tambotie.

'The archangel Lucifer? Guardian of Hell?' Primo repeated cautiously, recognizing nothing of the demonic in his visitor, yet sensing he had seen his face before. That he was supernatural there was no doubt; that he was angelic was also obvious, for his great wings, at rest against his back, reached from above his shoulders to the backs of his knees.

If his visitor was indeed the Devil, he was extra-ordinarily beautiful and serene. Perhaps, thought Primo, he was not the Devil himself but a minor, recently fallen angel in the Devil's service. Whatever the case, he realized that the invocation he had released to call Beatrice home had gone awry. He raced through its components, trying unsuccessfully to trace his error.

'I seem to have made a mistake – I was trying to call my wife back home. My wife has left me,' he said. 'I used a spell, an incantation I hadn't used before. I've been finding it lonely without her. I'm sorry to have disturbed you.'

Primo's visitor stood before him, majestically, with no hint of judgement or anger. Though not smiling, there was something in his look that touched Primo to the core. Feeling foolish, he continued, 'I'm not sure how to make amends. Is there something I can do to help you get back home?'

Yet even as he made the offer, he was filled with an overwhelming need to prevent this extraordinary being's departure. Why? He could not say. He knew only that, above all, he must delay his celestial visitor (he could not possibly be infernal) for as long as possible.

'But you are here! Have you come a great distance? Yes, you must have. Have a rest. Please, take a seat. Sit with me. Spend the afternoon. We can talk a bit. Are you busy? Must you rush off anywhere?'

'Not really,' replied the Devil. 'I have time enough.' He turned the kitchen chair, which Primo had pulled out for him, and sat sideways in it, so that his wings would not be crushed.

At that very moment, at Da Pasquale, twenty-four fruited breads, just out of the oven, were lined up on the kitchen's central work surface. All had an inexplicable bluish bloom to them and they tasted unaccountably bitter. Next to them lay as many salami *Fiorentini*, each cut down the centre and splayed for inspection. They too had a bluish tint and they tasted sour.

Pasquale, verging on hysteria, was pacing up and down, while in the background the high repeated notes of a flute in Johann Sebastian Bach's Cantata 8 carried an unnoticed but ominous charm. Lovemore and Dambudzo stood watching him, too shocked to speak – they had never known him to fail at anything in his kitchen. Beatrice, ashen, followed Pasquale as he strode, trying to console him, but he pushed her aside.

The delicatessen was shut and the blinds drawn. A sign announced unceremoniously: CLOSED.

ithin a week of the Devil's arrival, Primo's world had refreshed itself. Primo could not say exactly what his visitor had brought with him. He knew only that his life had changed for ever. It had a glow to it, as though a shaft of light had penetrated it. He had not brought up the subject of his visitor's true identity, but he was certain that he was no devil.

Primo set himself to cleaning the house, sweeping out the signs of misery and slothfulness that had settled after Beatrice left. He filled a vase with red chrysanthemums and placed it in the centre of the kitchen table. He polished his crystals, swept the back yard, watered the garden and the stoep plants, and trimmed the dead leaves from the violets.

The Devil had given him a robe. It was wrapped in papyrus and tied with plaited hemp. Primo, too moved to say anything, took it tentatively, first holding it to his chest, then opening it carefully. It was made of indigo tussore silk. A row of double chain-stitch ran from the shoulder line to the cuff of each sleeve.

When Primo put on the garment, he felt as though his skin had been wrapped in air, so light and unobtrusive was it. He turned a sleeve back and noticed that the seams had been stitched by hand.

Primo looked into the Devil's eyes, and they spoke back to Primo. They spoke as though they had sighed; as though they were darkened underground pools. They spoke of such depth, such purity and honesty, that Primo realized his visitor had told him no untruths. These were the eyes of truth itself. Primo felt shaken and confused, for that gaze conflicted with every religious notion of the Devil he had come across. Yet he acknowledged, in a hoarse whisper, 'Yes, you are Lucifer. God's Archangel. Lucifer, the Guardian of Hell.'

The Devil nodded and said, 'I am that one.'

'Why do you have two locked rooms?' asked the Devil, the next day. 'What do you keep inside them?'

'My past, I suppose,' replied Primo, without

135

looking up. 'One was my father's workshop and the other I shared with my aunt. I locked them both when they died.'

They were sitting at the kitchen table. Primo was servicing his telescope and had its parts spread out on a large square of red felt. He polished a lens.

'May I look inside?' asked the Devil.

'They've been closed for many years.'

'Things should not be left locked for ever.'

'Another time, then,' said Primo, uncomfortably.

'There is no time like the present.'

Primo lifted the lens to his eye and, turning towards the light, peered through it, then polished it again, saying nothing. Some moments passed.

'Well?' probed the Devil.

They had the radio on and were listening to the Soweto String Quartet, live in concert from the Grahamstown Festival. Violins threaded a trail of frenzied sound round the room, chasing the viola, halting in midair as the cello responded with sage slowness.

A bee, which had found its way into the kitchen during the day, struck repeatedly against the bare bulb, until the Devil stood up, cupped his hand around it and released it out of the window.

'I'll open one for you. You may look inside but then I'll have to lock it again.' Primo put the lens down, wiped his palms against his sides and switched off the radio. He walked to the lounge, opened the display cabinet and took two keys (the

old heavy latch-lock type) from the Susie Cooper
sugar bowl. He chose one and put the other away.

If he had stopped to look at the framed painting
hanging above the sideboard, he would have noticed
that the image of the third angel, the one with thick
mahogany curls, standing in the middle of the trio,
was no longer there. Only two angels sounded their
trumpets in *Aurora Triumphans*; only two put night
to sleep and wakened the dawn in the epic masterpiece.

With the Devil following, Primo made his way
down the passage to the sealed room on the 21A
side and unlocked it, pushing the door open before
him.

The room was spectacular for its stillness.
Though everything in it spoke of time,
mechanism and motion, nothing moved. Four
longcase clocks stood against the opposite wall.
Around them, placed side by side, their beautiful
dials seeming to gaze across the room, hung a collection of clocks: a French provincial *comtoise*, an
eighteenth-century tavern clock, a rare hooded wall
clock, several nineteenth-century bracket clocks
and two railway clocks. There was also a 1950s
kitchen clock with the Coca-Cola signature across its
face.

Five rows of pocket watches, some with their
chains, others without, hung in neat formation on
the second wall.

The third wall of the room was fitted with a large chest of many small drawers, each with a small brass handle and each filled, in order of size and type, with thousands of watch parts that Primo, as a child, had loved sorting on rainy days.

The surface of a workbench under the boarded-up window was lined with an assortment of mantel and table clocks of various vintages. Under the work-bench were stacked a number of wooden boxes and a leather suitcase which contained Primo's child-hood collection of clocks and watches.

A roll-top desk, its inner surface covered with small boxes of watchmakers' instruments, watch parts and a magnifying glass, lay open, as if waiting for its master to sit before it. A chair stood at a slight angle to the desk, as though he had just that moment stood up, pushed the chair back and left the room, intending to return. Draped on the back of the chair was a grey cardigan and on its seat a worn, embroidered cushion. A gossamer of dust covered everything.

Primo did not enter the room. He stood aside as the Devil stepped in, pushing away the cob-webs. The Devil surveyed the contents, his eyes resting for a while on a gold cherub standing atop an ornate cylindrical clock, baton in hand, in per-petual stillness, about to strike the hour against a gong.

He turned to Primo, who, standing at the threshold, felt the need to explain, saying, 'My father was obsessed with time. He believed that this bracket of time of which we are conscious is but a single thread of true time. He imagined that true time has innumerable dimensions; that there are ribbons of time running concurrently, like the warp and weft of cloth.

'My father was always seeking true time. He reasoned that if time were multidimensional, then history must unfold in countless ways. There was a certain period in his own past life, and that of my aunt, that he wanted to return to and divert along another route, so that what had happened to them would become another event. He wanted to change their own history.'

The Devil sat on the watchmaker's chair, picked up a gilt lantern clock, ran a finger around the fine filigree work and touched, one by one, at second intervals, each of the numerals of the hour.

Putting it down, he turned to face Primo and said, 'I think we should wind the clocks. Come, I will help you. We will wind them together.'

Trace smells of fine oil and camphor reminded Primo of boyhood days spent in this room. Memory rushed through him. He remembered his father's hands, his delicate fingers, the nails he always cut short, the gold band on his finger, the white cuffs sticking out from his jersey, his back bent over his work, his voice, his gentleness, his brown polished shoes, his grey tweed trousers, his canvas apron. Primo ran trembling hands through his hair and stepped into the world he had not entered for nearly twenty years.

Beginning with the longcase clocks, Primo and the Devil worked methodically and without speaking, winding and setting the mechanisms, swinging pendulums back into motion. It took most of the evening, and as they progressed the comforting music of Primo's childhood began to play again in various tones of ticking, tocking, striking, chiming, whirring, ringing and gonging. When, finally, every clock was active, they went back to the kitchen, leaving the door open so that the sounds of time filled the house once more. Somehow the bee had found its way in again. To stop its mad smacking against the bulb, the Devil switched off the kitchen light. A soft glow came through from the passages, and he and Primo stood in the semi-darkness, the innards of the telescope spread out on the table, twinkling in the half-light.

'Shall we go for a walk?' asked the Devil. 'The night is lovely.'

'Yes,' agreed Primo. 'I'll finish this in the morning.'

Pasquale's misfortune threw the Long Street community into disarray. They had already lost the services of their soothsayer, and now, to make matters worse, Da Pasquale, which had closed only once in its entire history – for a month when Massimo and Cornelia died – was permanently shut.

His regular patrons would gather at the door of Da Pasquale, hoping it would open, and that all would return to normal. They missed the simplest of things – a slice of bread topped with *mortadella* and artichokes; coffee with a slice of sweet almond cake. They missed the gossip and exchange of news.

The poker players left phone messages, wrote letters, sent e-mails and shouted up at Pasquale's balcony, to no avail. They were reluctant to play in any of Long Street's other clubs and restaurants, for none had the atmosphere and warmth they were accustomed to. None had Pasquale as host. They would cluster on the pavement in time for their Saturday night ten o'clock games, pacing, hands in pockets, kicking against the pavement, shuffling their cards, eventually moving on to play at Maginty's, but with a sense of loss and abandonment beating in their hearts. Lazar would arrive each evening with his violin and, finding the door locked, would stand outside, beneath the balcony, and play something for his dear friend, then make his sad way home.

On that appalling afternoon when his salami and fruited bread had 'blued', Pasquale, determined to get to the root of the problem without interference, sent Lovemore and Dambudzo home, though they argued and lamented bitterly, wanting to help him find the scourge.

Suspecting fungus, he threw all his stock into the

back alley – where street children and *bergies* fought over it – and he scrubbed down the entire kitchen and every utensil. Over the next fortnight, drinking vast quantities of Red Bull and sweet black coffee, he restocked his larder, then began making small batches of fruited breads and salami. He worked carefully, paying the utmost attention to every measure and every step. Even so, fruited breads came out of the oven bitter and the salami, even before their curing process had begun, expressed a sourness. And still the blue blush covered every-thing.

Pasquale grew increasingly frantic, unpredictable and impossible to reason with. He did not eat and lost weight rapidly, started to smoke and wept openly at the least provocation. Virginia showed no sympathy when Beatrice phoned her. 'So what's the problem?' she asked. 'What can I do about it? I've got my own things to deal with. Tell him to cook something else. Why stay hung up on damn bread and salami, for God's sake?'

ne night, alone in his partly lit shop, drunk on bourbon and slouched across a table, Pasquale had a vision. At the bar, with her back to him, her blue cape falling in pleats down to the floor, sat the Virgin Mary, lit up by her halo. Pasquale did not realize who she was and, think-ing her a customer who had come in for a drink, wondered how she had entered the locked premises.

Unsteadily, he rose to his feet and shakily addressed her, 'Madame, can't you read? We are closed. There is a sign on the door. Da Pasquale is closed. Will you be kind enough to go out the way you came in?'

The vision turned to face Pasquale and he saw, through a murk of caffeine and alcohol, a woman beautiful beyond description, radiating tranquillity and peace. She smiled, serenely, and he felt himself shrouded in benevolence. Her halo throbbed and in its light he recognized the baker's Holy Virgin whom his father had often spoken of.

'*Sacra Vergine!*' he gasped. 'You are real!'

As he said these words, the Mother of God smiled, then evaporated from his sight.

'No! No! I don't mean you to go! No! I am open for you! *Santa Maria!* Forgive me! Forgive me! I did not recognize you!'

Pasquale lunged towards the bar to apprehend her, grabbing at the counter, at the bar stool, for something left of her texture. But there was nothing of her to hold. She had disappeared. He slumped to the floor and wept like a baby.

The next morning, even though his head ached, Pasquale reflected on something his father had once told him, and in this way understood the Virgin's visitation of the night before. His father had said that the butcher and the baker were philosophers and that, in addition to travelling and cooking, they discussed theological matters and ethics. They revealed certain Catholic mysteries, among them the fact that the Virgin Mary, as the Mother of God, was a willing emissary when it came to sending prayers directly to the Divine ear.

How obvious, Pasquale reasoned. He must turn to her! She had come to tell him that he should call in the Catholics to bless him and his workspace, and that he must place her statue in his kitchen to overlook his work, as the baker had always done.

With single-mindedness, Pasquale set off to find a statue that looked exactly like the baker's. She would have a serene and beautiful, ageless face; she would be wearing a long white dress that did not lie against her body to reveal her womanly form. It would fall down in folds to her unshod, delicate and perfect feet, on each of which rested a pink rose. She would wear over her shoulders a long cape of the palest blue, its hood not quite concealing her hair; her arms would be stretched out, palms turned upwards; around her head would be a halo of gold.

First he turned to his long-time friend, Sack of Sack Antiques, and they searched his tightly packed basement storerooms. Sack regularly bought job-lots at auctions but, with no time to check through them, stored them away for later attention. Together they scoured the junk shops of Kalk Bay, Brooklyn and Goodwood. Pasquale questioned immigrant traders at Green Point market, hoping they might know of a statue looted from an Angolan or Mozambican mission. He sent Lovemore and Dambudzo to check on the vendors at the station, in the hope that a stolen statue had turned up among them. In the Catholic Bookshop he found only small cheap plastic ornaments of Our Lady of Lourdes, pressed by the thousand in Hong Kong. Finally, after days of searching, and on Sack's suggestion to ask at Catholic institutions, Pasquale found her. There, at Nazareth House, on a shelf in the lobby, stood a statue of the Virgin Mary, in all her grace and beauty.

Of course, the Mother Superior of the convent, Mother Clementina, could not sell her, or hire her out. What was Pasquale to do? He would have to tell her the truth, quite simply. This he did with such sincerity and anguish that Mother Clementina, who was nearing her sixtieth year in the holy order, was utterly charmed by this intense Jewish man before her. Even though she had chosen a life free of men, his fine looks were not lost on her.

'She was given to our convent by Mr Umberto Biccari, the father of the jeweller,' she explained, looking across her desk at Pasquale. 'He was a prisoner of war, captured in North Africa and interned at Zonderwater. He presented the statue some years later, when he had settled in Cape Town, as a way of saying thank you, I suppose, to God, for sparing his life, when so many of his comrades had died.'

Pasquale stood up and began pacing the small office as Mother Clementina spoke. He lit a cigarette and offered her one, too preoccupied to notice her smile when she declined. As he listened to her voice, he took in the things of the room – a vase of plastic flowers, a picture of the Sacred Heart, a crucifix on the wall behind her with the figure of Christ hanging in perpetual agony.

'Will the Biccari family mind if you lend me the statue?' he asked. 'I know Biccari the jeweller well – we have been friends for many years. And he is a regular customer of mine. I can ask him myself, if it makes things easier for you.'

'Of course they won't mind. I wonder whether they even know about the statue. Old man Biccari presented it before he married, before he had children. And, of course, the Biccari family is no longer Catholic – he married a Jewish girl. I'm quite sure that if Umberto Biccari were alive, he would allow me to let the statue stand in your kitchen for a while, to help you through your times of trouble.' She hesitated for a moment. 'You said earlier that your father was Italian. Was he also a prisoner of war?'

'No,' answered Pasquale. 'Not in the true sense. Not really. But he was confined. He hid with friends.'

'Ah, yes. I understand,' said Mother Clementina. 'Well now, let's take this chair through to the hall. If you stand on it, you'll reach her quite easily. She's rather heavy. But before you go, you might be interested to know her history. After his release, after war ended, Mr Biccari wrote home, to his family, and requested that they procure a statue. His sister found this one for sale at a market. You'll see, when you look at her closely, that the statue barely survived the war. Her cheek was grazed by a passing bullet, or perhaps a piece of shrapnel. Mr Biccari had the scar repaired.'

As Pasquale reached up for the statue, his eyes met with hers and he noted, with a slight shiver, how much they resembled the eyes of the Virgin Mary he had seen at his bar.

'Thank you, Mother Clementina,' he said, holding the statue. 'I will take great care of her, I assure you.'

'I know. I don't have to ask you to be mindful of her. I know she'll be in caring and safe hands.'

Mother Clementina watched Pasquale walk down the convent driveway with the beautiful statue in his arms, and smiled.

Not only did she agree to let the Virgin Mary take up temporary residence at Da Pasquale, she also asked Father Michael, the convent's priest, to bless the premises and deal with any Roman Catholic souls who, she reasoned, had got lost on their way to Purgatory and somehow become holed up at Da Pasquale to wreak havoc upon breads and salami.

*   *   *

ather Michael blessed Da Pasquale and sprinkled holy water in all corners. He sanctified and sent on their way the lost souls he believed, in agreement with Mother Clementina, to be at the root of the problem. Finally, after Pasquale had placed the statue on a shelf overlooking the kitchen, Father Michael recited what he held to be the most beautiful of prayers, the 'Hail, Holy Queen'. There was now nothing more to be done but for Pasquale to begin baking, to phone Lovemore and Dambudzo, and to let his friends and customers know that he was back at work. Confidently he pledged the first batch of fruited breads to the sisters and inmates of Nazareth House, and to Father Michael.

'Beatrice!' he called out, as he measured and weighed his ingredients. 'I haven't told you for some weeks that I love you! . . . Well, I love you! Can you hear me? Where are you? Are you drinking at the bar? Come here! Come eat some maraschino cherries. Come kiss me while I work!'

Beatrice was at the bar, laughing with Dr Baldinger, whom she had just let in. 'No,' she called out. 'I've opened up for a customer. I'm busy. I know you love me, Pasqui. But I'm drinking with the good Doctor. Save me the cherries for later! If we come through to you, you'll get your ingredients confused.'

'Yes, Pasquale,' said Dr Baldinger. 'Let the dear Beatrice serve me. Your delicatessen has not seen a customer for so long. Let us take a little drink of liqueur. You get on there with your baking. We'll come through to taste the finished products later.'

Beatrice put on a Celedonio Romero cassette and Da Pasquale filled with the dulcet sounds of guitar. She stood smiling across the bar at Dr Baldinger and he beamed back at her as they listened for a moment to Pasquale hard at work, singing and eulogizing his ingredients. Then they walked through to his kitchen and sat on high stools while he got on with his creation. The sweet smile of the Virgin Mary gave an added feeling of joy to the kitchen.

But, after hours of preparation and baking, when Pasquale opened the oven he immediately saw that the problem was still with him, for blue vapours permeated the hot air. He threw himself down against the counter and wept, howling in madness. His heart was broken. He made his way upstairs and sat forlornly on the balcony, his face in his hands, trembling.

'Do you think the time is right now, to open the second locked room?' asked the Devil.

Primo looked up from the light meal he was eating: ricotta sprinkled with fresh dill, slices of ripe tomato, a trickle of olive oil, a trace of balsamic vinegar, crushed garlic. They had fires burning in both the deep fireplaces and this radiated warmth throughout the house. 'Yes,' he agreed. 'It's probably time now. But let me finish eating first. I need to work up some courage.' He smiled sheepishly and broke a small loaf in half. Thoughtfully picking up crumbs and placing them on his tongue, 'Are you sure you don't want to eat anything?' he said.

'Quite sure,' replied the Devil as he traced a finger over the cross-stitch flowers of the tablecloth.

When Primo had finished, he cleared the table, took the key from the display cabinet and led the way down the second passage.

He unlocked the door and pushed it open, switched on the light and stepped in, the Devil behind him. The room, simply furnished and almost empty in comparison with his father's workshop, smelt musty.

Two single old-fashioned iron beds, their mattresses slightly sunken, were covered with candlewick spreads. One, Primo's, was pale blue and one, his aunt's, pink. Each had, at its foot, a folded crocheted rug. On the pink bed rested a worn teddy bear, its head drooped at a questioning angle, its button eyes still bright, its black nose missing.

Except for a cupboard and a trunk, there was no other furniture. Above the blue bed hung a framed sepia photograph of a beautiful young woman holding a baby, with a handsome man at her side. This was Primo's mother, with him in her arms and his father beside her. A lump of anguish settled in Primo's throat and he felt his eyes smart with the threat of tears.

Primo had shared this room with his aunt until he was twenty-five years old, until he had married Beatrice and moved to her flat. Had he remained a boy that long? Had his childhood run on and on, intruding into his manhood? he wondered now as he looked around the room, remembering how his aunt had wanted to rearrange the house so as to accommodate Beatrice, rather than let Primo leave. She and his father, holding back tears and overwhelmed by an uncontrollable fear that they might not see him again, had watched him pack a single suitcase of clothes.

'He must live his life,' Eugenio had said on their first night without Primo, in their house which now felt so empty without him.

'Yes,' Lidia had repeated, enunciating each word. 'He must live his life.'

The Devil sat on the blue bed and pointed at the trunk at the side of the closed wardrobe. Without a word Primo knelt beside it and opened it. The sickly smell of old trapped naphthalene escaped. He lifted out the contents: three plain blouses with buttons down the front; a couple of simple pleated skirts; two cardigans; the elegant suit and beret his aunt had worn when she left Italy for Africa – and to his wedding. These were the garments of a modest, humble woman. He had forgotten that he had folded her clothes and packed them away, after her death, after their deaths. It had been like dreaming, then; putting away for ever what had once been part of people, on that cold night, not unlike tonight, when the ice wind was blowing, as it was now, when in disbelief that they had died and left him, he had closed the doors to the lives of his father and aunt, and locked them away.

He lifted from the trunk a book of Italian fairy tales, a biscuit tin containing unused embroidered handkerchiefs, a bundle of crochet hooks, some balls of wool; a few crochet squares that had been the start of a new blanket. Here was his aunt's whole life.

He reached deeper into the trunk and lifted out household linen wrapped in tissue paper, so old that the paper crumbled as he touched it. He brushed it to the floor, where it settled like huge flakes of dirty snow. The embroidered linen had formed his aunt's trousseau.

The Devil took the folded cloth from Primo's hands. The linen was no longer white but yellowed and rust-marked. As the Devil opened it out to see it better, it fell apart at the foldlines, which had perished. Primo continued to unpack tissue-wrapped linen and pile it between himself and the Devil, on the bed. Neither spoke. The Devil was engrossed in the stitches, the precise and delicate designs. He picked up a sampler and checked each line of work. Here were some unusual stitches and he studied their route through the symmetrical weave of the linen.

'This is very beautiful embroidery,' he said. 'Your

aunt was a good needlewoman. It seems such a pity these things were put away. Why did she never use them?' He placed the linen neatly back in the trunk with the flakes of tissue, which he carefully picked up.

Primo could not answer, for he knew very little about his aunt – she had never spoken about herself. He could tell the Devil that she had been a teller of enchanting stories, that his parents had allowed her to choose his name and that she loved him as though he were her own son.

He could also report that his aunt – like his father – had been a survivor of Auschwitz, that she bore a tattooed number on her left arm, that she suffered regular nightmares and that she was a widow.

The truth is, Primo's aunt was not a widow. She had never married.

In the rainy early-morning darkness of 16 October 1943, during the sixth week of the German occupation of Italy, SS police sealed off Rome's old Jewish ghetto. Armed guards fired shots and pounded on doors, demanding that all Jews come into the streets, to be herded into waiting trucks and transported to a detention centre at the military college, not far from the Vatican City. There they remained under guard for a few days before being trucked to the cargo-loading platform of Tiburtina station (bypassing the passenger terminal) and pressed into freight cars for deportation to

Auschwitz. Twenty-year-old Eugenio Verona and his twin sister, Lidia, did not escape this first massive, carefully planned round-up.

When the heavy door of the freight car crashed shut and gloom descended – the only light came through a high, narrow barred slot – Lidia could barely move, and she found it hard to breathe in the crush of prisoners crammed around her. She could not see where her brother was, did not know whether he was squashed against the splinter-filled sides of the car, whether he had fallen and was now gasping in the trample of feet. She hoped he had made a dash down the platform and escaped.

Lidia's long plait kept catching between her back and someone's body. Against her shoulder pressed a face; against her side pressed a shoulder; into her lower back pressed an arm. Her own body was pushed against that of a man, so closely that she could feel his form – his thighs, his chest, his face, unshaven for some days. She could smell his acrid sweat and his dry breath, sour from thirst. The body of this man received hers, and stopped her from falling.

In the darkness, the voice of the man whose body allowed hers to rest began to whisper. 'I will tell you stories, *signorina*, while we journey,' it said. 'I will tell you stories of knights who ride their white horses, at slow pace, through all our histories, through all time, bearing a flaming torch of light to illumine the darkness, to show us the way through human ignorance.

'I will tell you of angels who visit us in our darkest hour, of how they caress our weakened limbs and breathe into our tormented souls. I will tell you stories, and you must listen to my voice, and not to the groaning in your throat, nor to the sighing in your heart.'

The voice of this man was soft and unobtrusive, yet it rose above the clickety-clack of the train labouring over the tracks, above the rasp of metal on metal. The voice filled time-present so completely that it carried her into imagery beyond the confines of the freight car. Because of it she would never recall the sordid details of the dark journey from Rome through Orte, Florence, and Padua, through Austria and Germany, and into Poland, where the entrance to Auschwitz waited like the portals of Dante's hell. She would forget the crush in the freight car, its floor awash with excrement and vomit, its walls marked with the blood of hands and faces that scraped against them. She would forget the futile disputes, the curses, the agitation, the cramped aching of people crushed together in so small a space.

Her memory would begin only when the train reached its final destination, when the doors of its carriages slammed open and the human cargo disembarked into a night lit by harsh floodlights and guarded by armed soldiers with dogs. From there she would remember her trembling legs, her throat cracked by thirst and how it was now her turn to help her companion, for he could barely walk. She would remember finding Eugenio in the confused and silent crowd, and touching him briefly. She would remember being separated from the men, herded off with young women. She would hold in her mind for ever the horror of the hell she had just entered.

Above all of this, imprinted in her memory would be the stories the stranger had told her. And his name: Primus.

Eugenio Verona had never once doubted that he would survive Auschwitz. His anger, his sense of violation, his disgust at the depths to which humans could sink – these were all factors which strengthened his will to live. If he survived, so too, he believed, would his sister; after all, they had been conceived and born together.

After more than a year of living through the grotesque; of being courted by death and finding reprieve; of seeing his emaciated fellows shorn of their dignity, forced to animate a monstrous drama of filth, disease and barbarism, an end to the nightmare finally came. In the early days of January 1945, with the Russian front rapidly advancing, the Germans ordered a mass evacuation of Auschwitz and its satellite camps. Some twenty thousand prisoners, clad only in their mean and ragged prison suits and ill-fitting wooden clogs, were set on a gruelling march towards Buchenwald and Mauthausen, while the ill and weak were abandoned to their fate. (History would record that the column of evacuees vanished, almost in its entirety.)

Eugenio, among the prudent few, hid, and so escaped the march and certain death. He found Lidia, abandoned, barely recognizable, wasted, burning with scarlet fever in the hospital barracks.

When the first Russian patrol came in sight of the camp, Eugenio was one of the first to see it. Four young soldiers rode up on horseback and stopped at the barbed-wire fence. Perched on their horses, saying nothing, they merely surveyed the dead sprawled across the cold yard, and the few still-living emaciated human forms. To Eugenio it seemed that four archangels, their cheeks rosy from the cold, had ridden in to redeem him and his sister. Four archangels wrapped in fur and thick coats, bearing Sten guns – not flaming swords – and riding horses that snorted white steam into the cold air, stood solemnly at the perimeter of hell. Eugenio made his way back to the barracks where his twin lay close to death and, cupping his hands around her hollow face, forced her to find the will to live.

(Primo would never know what the stars and planets had really meant to his father. Eugenio had not disclosed, when teaching his son to view and understand the explosion of starlight and stardust through their Kloof Street skylight, that he imagined this to be the Diaspora of his fellow inmates at Auschwitz.)

After liberation, Eugenio and Lidia had made their arduous way back to Rome and tried to reconstruct a semblance of their former lives. Eugenio helped his sister search for her story-teller, though she did not know who he was. She knew only his first name. Together they read the list of survivors' names that was posted outside the synagogue and regularly updated, hoping, because it was an unusual name – the Latin Primus rather than the Italian Primo – to find it included. It was a fruitless search. So many people had disappeared, so many identities had been erased, that it was impossible to trace a person without knowing his full name.

In the freight car, Primus had said nothing about himself. He had only recited stories, and told her that he had witnessed the confiscation of Rome's Jewish library. 'I believe', he had whispered, 'that what is written, what is given to the world in literature, exists for ever. Though the books and parchments be burnt or shredded, the author has created and given lore, so it exists in humanity's collective soul. No bonfire of pages, no torching of script, can extinguish lore. Ever.'

Perhaps he was a librarian, perhaps a published author, perhaps a publisher. Eugenio explored all these possibilities for his sister, standing alongside her while she described her lost friend, as best she could, to publishers, writers' associations, newspaper editors, survivors who worked at Jewish institutions. It was useless to say that he had been wearing a light-coloured suit – a tailor-made suit (she knew this from the stitching on the lapels which she had felt with her fingertips) – because everyone, on entering the camp, had been stripped of their own clothing and dressed in degrading prison garb.

She could have identified him by his voice, which was soft and narcotic. It was a voice like web-fine threading that wound itself about her, enchanting her and lifting her away from time-present. But this was no help in her search for him.

It became clear to Eugenio that the man named Primus, his sister's storyteller, the man who had helped her through the first stage of their nightmare, had not himself survived Auschwitz. He did not express his view, though, not wanting to crush Lidia's hope.

Finally he decided they should emigrate, leave the sorrows of post-war Italy, and begin a new life in Africa. He packed for both of them, and they travelled first to the Belgian Congo, then to Southern Rhodesia and finally settled in Cape Town. Here he met and married an Afrikaans girl, Susanna le Roux, and set up house for his wife and sister. Unable to secure work, he apprenticed himself to a watchmaker before opening his own workshop in the front room of their home.

In central Africa, Lidia had found the heat unbearable and was afraid of the wide openness. In Cape Town she made no effort to meet people or make friends. She stayed indoors and began to embroider a dowry of household and bed linen. Eugenio bought her yards of first-grade cotton and linen and these she measured out, cut and hemmed as top sheets and under sheets, pillow slips and bed covers, table and tray cloths, serviettes and runners. In the top right-hand corner of each item she embroidered her initials, entwined with those of the storyteller: *LV & P*. She used white cottons, working some in drawn thread and satin stitch and others in split-stitch, cross-stitch, Cretan, feather and twisted chain. When each piece of work was complete, she wrapped it in tissue and placed it in a trunk with a few mothballs.

When their son was born, Eugenio and Susanna allowed Lidia to name him Primo, after her storyteller. From his first day of life Lidia told the baby his namesake's stories, cradling him in her arms, for the last thing the storyteller had said to her was: 'Promise me that you will live. Promise me that my stories will live.'

She had promised.

Primo had shared his aunt's bedroom because she was haunted by nightmares. Even though they slept with the passage light on so there was always a glow to the room, she did not want to wake up and find herself alone. When he was very little she had shared the bed with him, holding him close to herself, for it gave her comfort to feel his warm baby breath against her and to hear his heart beating, urgent for life. When he grew taller and needed his own bed, she kept the beds close together, so she could hold his hand through the night, with her fingers on the pulse of his wrist.

Sometimes, when he was older and he had moved the beds apart, he would be woken by her soft crying and, frightened by her night terrors, would lie very still. There were times when she would call out to him, call him by his Latin name, Primus, and he would go over to her bed in the semi-darkness and hold her hand, trying to comfort her, though she was still asleep. As the years passed, she called out less and less, though she still wept or whimpered, late in the night.

When he was a grown man he never questioned that they should still share a room, for he had comforted her throughout his life, and it never occurred to him that it was not his role to guide her out from the darkness of her horrors. If she cried out, he would sit at her bedside and tell her the stories she had told him as a child. Even though his soft voice never woke her, it seemed to soothe her nightmare, for she would moan something incomprehensible, then breathe evenly, roll over and sleep peacefully.

*   *   *

lthough Primo's sense that evil might be a more powerful force than good was seeded by his father and aunt, it had taken root from his own observations of life, particularly during his time spent with Pasquale in military service in Angola.

When, on leaving school, both young men had received their military call-up, their fathers had stood alone, Eugenio on his stoep, Massimo on his balcony, to wrestle with the fact that they would be betraying their children by allowing them to become soldiers and go to war. Each father had learnt that war offered no redemption – it either took lives or it inscribed them indelibly with the death of others. Each grappled with the inevitability of war, with the right-or-wrong of handing over to the military the first-born, not knowing whether the son would return, certain only that the bonny youth who marched forth would not be the man who returned.

They anguished over whether they were true South Africans, whether the wars of their adoptive country should be theirs, as Italians, as Europeans who had already had their share of war. Could they answer for their sons, each asked himself, who were born on this African soil? Should they pack up everything and leave? Flee? Return to Europe where there was no apartheid to defend, no *swart gevaar*, no enthroned Nationalist Party that decreed every white youth be handed over to the military or face imprisonment.

Both Eugenio and Massimo, each in his own way, had called out to the God of War, had summoned from their mythologies and religion the commander of that energy which compelled men to war, set one upon the other. But the God of War had merely hissed at them and left them to wrestle alone with their guilt as they waved their sons goodbye in the company of hundreds of parents at Cape Town station. They stood on the platform with Virginia and Beatrice watching the train, young shorn men leaning out of its windows and waving, snake its way out of sight towards the training camps where their sons would be taught that the enemy was black; that the enemy was a communist; that the enemy would kill white women and children; that the enemy was pouring over the borders of Angola and Mozambique; that white South African youth had the duty and honour to enter those countries and destroy those who would otherwise destroy them.

After their training, Primo and Pasquale were sent to Angola, to the bush which spread out before them in an elegance of wilderness, coloured with the luteous dryness of savannah, filled with birds and beasts and insects they had not known before, as city boys. They were at first deluded by this vast beauty. It did not appear to be a war field, a place where plunder and death could hold sway. This deception was short-lived, however, and their naïvety overturned.

They had been attached to a reconnaissance group of seasoned soldiers. This group was inflamed by an earlier ambush in which three of their company had been killed. The soldiers entered a native village in curved formation, Primo and Pasquale at the flanks. The village seemed deserted, still, like a picture-postcard before them, with three old men sitting on a log outside a hut, in the morning sun.

As the group of soldiers advanced, the old men rose shakily to their feet, lifting their hands in the air. They called out in Portuguese – a greeting, a surrender, a supplication. The soldiers paid no heed. They swung their automatic rifles in a mowing movement and fire rattled out, puncturing the old men, opening them so that their innards burst forth in a mess of blood as they fell.

Primo watched as, all in slow motion – for time had seemed to stretch, allowing him to witness every detail of the encounter – Pasquale and the others turned to crazed men, screaming and cursing as the forces of killing seized them. He was aware of himself frozen, his rifle heavy, his arms hanging and limp, unable to stop the killing, unable to call the group to sanity. Primo had noticed, as the massacre unfolded, that the old men's ribs pro-truded, so emaciated were they, and that their legs were thin and bent like sticks. One of the men had wet himself.

When they searched the village, they found no one. 'It is a village of old dead men,' Primo had whispered. Later he would remember thinking, I am one of a pack of mad dogs.

The next day the group came across a deserted village, which they searched for enemy soldiers. They found an ill old woman, lying on a reed mat in the darkness of her hut, with no possessions except a clay pot of brown water. A small boy lay with her. Primo's fellow soldiers shot them both in a rain of bullets. Then they caught a young woman, the child's mother, he presumed, and tore her apart, as a pack of starving dogs would tear a weakened foal. Inside a second deserted hut, a basket of grain was stabbed with a rifle butt and the golden kernels spilt across the ground. (Like the sun weeping, Primo had later reflected.) An enamel bowl was kicked across the yard. A lactating dog, her teats pendulous between her wire-thin legs, was shot. Goats bleated in terror and ran away. The huts were torched.

That night, when they reached base camp, Primo had to guard a deep pit in which prisoners, brought in by another reconnaissance group, were held, some of them wounded. They had no water and were naked. The heat of the day had sucked them of their life force, so they lay languid and parched and mostly silent, though the wounded ones groaned and one cried out occasionally. Primo had thrown his water bottle to them and later his ration pack. He sat under the quarter moon, in the great depth of the Angolan bush, as the sounds of crickets and night birds filled the air, mindful that the theatre of war had seized him as an unwilling extra and that there was no easy way to walk off the stage – not until the curtain was drawn closed and the orchestra of evil stopped playing. They had dressed him up for battle, the brigadiers and commandants and the generals of Pretoria, and sent him to act out their murders for them.

On that same night, Pasquale had his first dance with madness. He started sobbing like a child. Then he began tearing around, shooting and screaming, until someone knocked him unconscious with a rifle butt.

Under the stars Primo emptied his rifle clip of its bullets. He never reloaded it. If death confronted him, he reasoned, death could lead him away. He would never kill.

Primo had expressed to the Devil his idea that evil might be the greater force, and asked his opinion. It was a mild day in late winter, when early spring warmth had taken away the sharpness of the cold, encouraging new leaves to bud and bulbs to waken. They were in the study, Primo sitting deep in the armchair at the window, the Devil standing, paging through Dante's *Divine Comedy*.

'Dante never met me – in his earthly life, that is,' he said, putting the book aside and turning to face Primo. 'He wrote this epic without any knowledge of Hell in the Afterlife. His descriptions are quite inaccurate. God has not set up places of torture. The Divine does not demand punishment for earthly sin and has not tasked me to inflict eternal punishment.'

'You don't punish?'

'Of course not.'

'Then, who does?'

'No one. There is no punishment. There is only containment. Containment of the evil energies that human souls bring with them to the Afterlife.'

Primo held a mug of coffee between his hands, close to his face, savouring its warmth. 'Then, what exactly is it that you do?' he asked.

'In the Afterlife, you mean? Or here?'

'In the Afterlife, really. But also here.'

'I am an embroiderer,' said the Devil, smiling and running his hand across the stitches covering the front of his robe, touching lightly with his middle finger a line of silver-threaded Romanian couching. 'I embroider the garments of angels, their robes. I also restore old celestial tapestries and weavings.'

Primo stared at him, not sure whether the Devil was teasing.

'Look at my fine work! Come. Feel this texture.'

Primo's eyes followed the Devil's finger as it traced the stitching across his yoke and down a sleeve. He put his hands out, tentatively, and ran them down the Devil's arms, feeling the raised stitches against the soft linen. Each sleeve was a field of stem, double and bullion knots worked in purples and olive greens.

'I embroider while I watch over Hell,' continued the Devil. 'That is my work. I am the guardian of Hell in the Afterlife. I keep watch.'

'So what happens in Hell – in the Afterlife, that is – if it is not a place of punishment?' Primo asked.

'Nothing of importance,' replied the Devil. 'People just while away the time. We have clubs there, smoking dens and casinos. Most tend to play cards or gamble.' His eyes were glowing with mirth. 'But there are some who choose to pass their time more constructively.'

'I'm confused,' said Primo.

'Yes,' said the Devil. He flexed his wings slightly, then sat down, sideways, on the typist's chair and swivelled slowly, to the left and to the right. 'So let me explain. It is a fairly straightforward matter.

'Evil is indeed the greater force. There is no equipoise, no balance between it and good. Evil is not something set up as an opposite energy to that of the Divine. It is a singular force born and nurtured in the human soul.

'When the human soul crosses to the Afterlife, if it brings its evil with it, that evil must be contained or it will contaminate. The task ascribed to me is to see to the containment of human evil; I safeguard those destructive energies.

'For this I have divided Hell into two levels, the

Underworld and the Deep. I separate those human souls who are merely bad from those who are truly evil. The truly evil are kept in the Deep – they may never leave. The merely bad are kept in the Under-world, where they bide their time until they become good. Then they may move on to the next levels of the Afterlife.

'There are many who choose to stay on in the Underworld. For some it is a time of perpetual recreation. They aspire to nothing higher.

'There are also those who choose to stay with me. They enjoy my company.'

The Devil spread his wings their full span, twinkling in gold dust, then drew them in. 'You are smiling,' he said. 'Do you think I jest?'

'No. It just seems so . . . what word should I use? . . . so *unexpected*. So simple.'

'Yes, it is simple. Except that there is another Hell, a third Hell, that I watch over, one that is indeed terrible. It is here on earth. It is considered to be the true Hell. There you find Dante's torture, the scorched air, the dismembering, the death of beauty. This third Hell is war – it is the battleground where the human soul wages war. It is the scared earth, the fields of those dying at the hands of others, the bombed and burning cities.

'I am the Archangel who circles the diabolic land-scape of battle, the one who holds back the conflagration of war, who holds back the flames of human conflict, so they do not spread out of the confines of this earthly time. I draw the firewalls, as though they be curtains, to shut the inferno in where it belongs, so it spills not out. For this I am called the Angel of Dresden.

'I am alone in my work with fire. No other helps me. And it is an almost impossible task that I am assigned. You must agree. For the flames spread furiously. Your father was correct. Time is webbed and woven. So the fires of human warring can easily spread out and through all the levels. Were I to leave the war fields and the burning ravaged cities unattended, the whole universe, as known to the human mind, could combust. Can you imagine the conflagration? It would be beyond Dante's wildest imaginings!'

Primo, well versed in discourse, and never without a point of view or an argument, now found himself completely at a loss for words. He had listened intently to the Devil's description, absorbing its every detail, yet was unable to respond, so stunned was he by what he heard.

There was silence between them. Primo tried to search the Devil's eyes, to read the language that his angelic form spoke as he sat, still sideways on the typist's chair, his leather-clad feet placed firmly on the ground, his great wings at rest. His form spoke of dignity and nobility, as it always did; and his eyes of depth and compassion and infinite wisdom.

Were you there with me that day, my friend, thought Primo, when I was in the battle field? When my fellow soldiers shot the old woman and the child? Did you watch the old men die like dogs? Did you hold the flames of that burning village, Lucifer? Did you hear the wounded child scream as the fire caught him? Did you lift him from the flames, when I could not?

Still neither spoke. The Devil seemed to wait for Primo and his thoughts.

'Why has God given you this terrible task?' Primo asked, finally. 'Why do you alone safeguard the fires of human conflict? Why has the Divine thrown you into the midst of our destructions and hatred?' Are you not his favourite angel? he thought. As you would be mine, were I God. Should he not keep you at his right hand, as I would?

'We have each a task,' said the Devil. 'This is mine. Thus is my name Lucifer, Light Bearer. Light in its pure form, as you know, is fire.'

Some days later, Primo and the Devil were in the back garden, sitting under the mulberry tree. Primo had always believed war to be the most demeaning of human activities. Now he felt a deep shame, shame for his own kind, shame for what this angelic being had had to witness since the dawn of time, for war, he reflected, has always been man's brother in life.

War has walked alongside us, thought Primo, looking at the Devil. It has walked as our domesticated dogs and sheep and goats have, loyal to us, sleeping outside our dwellings, waiting for us to wake, never falling behind but keeping pace with us as we walk through time. And you have been there too, as a warden of our folly.

How is it for you, to witness brother battling against brother? For we are all brothers – are we not seeded from the same cosmologies and borne upon the same testaments?

Are you present at all our conflicts? Do you witness them, right at the front? When we are gallant silver knights on horseback? When we are warriors plundering and slaying? When we dig trenches and fill them with our poets? When we march our children ahead of us to do our killing?

Were you at Hiroshima, the greatest of our conflagrations, that multiple incineration where we lost what small innocence we had?

Or do you only come to our fires afterwards, after we have done our filthy deeds? When the music is stilled and all art turned to nothing?

The Devil faced the sun, enjoying its warmth. The surrounding low branches of the mulberry tree, with their new small-budding emerald green leaves, seemed to hold him.

There was a knock at the door.

'It's probably one of my clients,' replied Primo to the Devil's questioning glance, but making no move to answer. 'We'll just ignore it and they'll go away.'

'Is that the right response? Should we not open

the door?' asked the Devil, as the person knocked a second time. 'Perhaps you are needed.'

'Everyone needs me. But as I told you and as I try to tell them, I have retired. I don't want to deal with their everyday issues any more. I feel I have moved on,' said Primo.

'Answer this one. I am curious. I would like to see who it is,' said the Devil.

At the third knock Primo asked, 'How will I introduce you? As Lucifer?'

'You will not need to introduce me. I will not be visible.'

They walked down the passage, Primo without enthusiasm, for he had become protective of his privacy and felt irritated that their discussion had been interrupted. It was with reluctance that he unlocked the door.

Leaning against a pillar stood Virginia, smoking, wearing a tight, short black dress and knee-high black boots.

'Contessa, what can I do for you?' greeted Primo, without warmth or interest.

She threw her cigarette down and put it out with the tip of her boot. Frowning deeply and without greeting him, she said, 'Primo, I know you've stopped working, and I'm sorry to trouble you, but I need you to do a reading for me. Only one. I have to clarify something. It shouldn't take you long.'

The Devil nudged Primo, who in turn gestured to Virginia to enter, then followed her into his consulting room. She tossed a bundle of notes into the bronze urn and sat at the round table. Primo lit all the candles and a stick of incense. The room was darkened by the thick velvet curtains but glowed warmly in the candlelight.

Virginia looked unusually unkempt and tousled, as though she had been crying. There was the sickly sweet smell of alcohol on her breath. Her hair fell forward and she kept flipping it backwards off her face with an affected movement. She sat with her legs slightly apart. The dress crept up her thighs and Primo could see the small black triangle of her underwear. A strap slipped, exposing a pale shoulder on which was tattooed a red rose.

Primo, with the Devil standing next to him, lifted the cover from his crystal ball, rubbed it and waited. Both looked into it as, out of its opaqueness, a convex drama emerged:

> A seated man smokes a cigar; a glass of whisky is balanced on one knee, a woman is perched on the other.
> The woman throws her head from side to side, laughing;
> The man pulls the dress off her shoulders, kisses a breast;
> A door bursts open.
> A dishevelled woman enters, takes a pistol from her bag and discharges three bullets.

A fountain of scarlet blood spurts from the torso
of the man.
A trickle of crimson oozes from the right breast
of the woman.
Both fall to the floor.

Primo grimaced and glanced at the Devil, who then walked round to stand behind Virginia and place his palms over her eyes, closing them. She lifted a hand as though to brush something away, a cobweb perhaps, but her arm fell to her side. Her head dropped gently to her chest. She was asleep. The Devil lifted the limp arm and settled it on Virginia's lap, then returned to look again into the crystal ball.

'This is sordid. We shouldn't have let her in,' complained Primo.

'Do you generally reveal this sort of foreknowledge?' asked the Devil, not responding to Primo's judgements.

'No,' replied Primo. 'I never do.'

The Devil was silent, looking across at the slumbering Virginia. 'When I rouse her, you should caution her against violence.'

A dribble of saliva trickled down Virginia's chin. The Devil suggested they go for a walk.

They strolled all the way up Kloof Street, until they came to the ruins of the old orphanage. Here they sat under the gnarled wide-spreading oaks, looking across the city at the smooth curve of Table Bay.

The Devil, with his eyes closed, sat sideways against an oak, listening to the rush of fluids within its trunk and to its leaves murmuring.

Primo wanted to probe deeper into the mysteries the Devil had presented, but did not disturb him in his musing.

If I could paint, he thought, I would paint your image as I see it now – your wings sparkling like the pink pearl of shells, your long curls the red of cedar wood, your robe the violet-blue of evening. I would capture you for ever, with your shadow which is light, not darkness.

How does the fire of war not burn you, not scorch or blister you – you who are named for Dresden?

How do you hold flames without their terrible testimony marking your beauty, your countenance?

The Devil opened his eyes and turned to face Primo. A shaft of afternoon sunlight danced on him.

Do you read my mind? thought Primo. Do you read my offer? I will come with you. I will guard the flames with you. I will hold back the walls of fire, so you need keep lone watch no more.

'We can go back now. The day is getting late,' said the Devil, standing and shaking out his wings.

'Yes,' agreed Primo, though he wanted to stay.

*   *   *

fter his disastrous failure, Pasquale hauled a box of brandy upstairs and went to bed, where he swilled his way into an alcoholic temper. The room was littered with empty bottles, the bed wet with perspiration, brandy and vomit. He became abusive – shouting and swearing every time Beatrice came into the room. She was in despair and wanted to go home, but didn't know how to leave. For some strange reason, she felt responsible. Perhaps she distracted him; perhaps he could not focus on his work now that he was attending so vigilantly to her. If she had unleashed this storm, she reasoned, then she must stay until it blew itself out. She also didn't know how to explain to Primo what had happened.

She decided to clean the room, but as she entered he hurled a bottle at her. Narrowly missing, it shattered against the wall, leaving a splash of brandy-gold running down to the floor. Later he staggered downstairs, naked and thin, trembling and weeping. He went into the kitchen, took the statue of the Virgin Mary from its shelf and, pushing Beatrice out of his way as she tried to stop him, smashed it to the floor. He then locked himself in the larder.

Sobbing, Beatrice crept on her hands and knees towards the broken pieces of china and began to pick them up – a cheekbone, her beautiful mouth, a thumb and index finger, a rose, a fold of the blue robe. The now sorrowed eyes stared deeply at

Beatrice, as her mother had done, lying on her bed at the Blue Lodge, broken by anguish, torn apart by feelings of abandonment.

'Frankie,' Beatrice cried, clutching the shards as she made her way to the bar and phoned Dr Baldinger, barely coherent.

ovemore and Dambudzo lived behind the Railway Hotel in Woodstock with a group of fellow Zimbabweans.

When Pasquale had sent them home they could not accept that he had closed the delicatessen. They kept reporting in for work each morning, to be confronted by the closed front door and drawn blinds of Da Pasquale. They would let themselves in the back way with their own key, get news from Beatrice of the latest developments, and return to Woodstock and another day of worry.

One evening, at home, smoking pensively in the courtyard, Lovemore announced to Dambudzo, 'Mr Pasquale has magic on him. There is someone who wants Mr Pasquale to die.'

'No! It is not possible. White people do not do the magic to kill one another. Mr Pasquale is sick,' responded Dambudzo.

'I know white people do not do the killing magic. But when they are dead, they are too clever and then they can do it. This magic is from the cook from the Montebello hotel. You remember the one who went to court and said Mr Pasquale stole his recipe? He killed himself, you remember that? He threw himself out from BP Building. Now his spirit is coming back to fetch the recipe. That is why all the cooking goes wrong in the kitchen. He can't find the recipe, so he kills Mr Pasquale slowly. That is why Mr Pasquale is so thin. We must stop that jealous cook, or Mr Pasquale will surely die.'

The next day Lovemore and Dambudzo took a taxi out to Khayalitsha and after some enquiries found, in a shack behind the Oliver Tambo Centre, a Xhosa woman practising as a *gqira* – a traditional healer. They were not sure of her credibility – she was not wearing the beads and animal-skin headdress which a Shona *n'anga* would have worn. Nor did she have the wide variety of dried herbs, desiccated organs and pulverized animal parts they were accustomed to seeing in healers' huts back home. They chose not to use her services.

On returning to Woodstock they consulted their fellow Zimbabweans and between them came up with a partial solution. They would have to appease the spirit of the Montebello's dead chef themselves and cancel his vendetta, so that he left Pasquale alone and stopped tampering in the kitchen; and they would have to protect Pasquale from the spell which was sapping his life force, until such time as they located a Shona diviner to remove it permanently.

So as not to alert the evil-doing spirit to their plan, they waited for a night of no moon, and worked by candlelight in their courtyard. Meticulously following Pasquale's recipe, they grated a carrot, chopped up spring onions, a leek and celery leaves (all very finely); and simmered these with crushed garlic in virgin olive oil. When all was glassy, and the good mingled smells rose from the pot, they added skinned and chopped very ripe bell tomatoes, fresh sweet basil and origanum, a splash of red wine, ground black pepper and sea salt. The mixture was left to cook slowly on a gas stove. When it was done – thick and red and rich – they added eight anchovy fillets, a teaspoon of salted capers and a cup of pitted black olives before folding it into maize meal simmering in an iron pot, standing on hot coals. The thick blend, which Lovemore and Dambudzo stirred rhythmically and in turn, heaved heavily. As each big bubble of the maize porridge burst and released a hiss of aromatic steam, friends beat on a hide drum and twanged at an *mbira*.

The utterly delicious fragrance of *polenta alla Madiba* filled the air and rose up into the spirit world to search for the unsuspecting soul of Riaan Kotze, and appease him.

Lovemore chuckled to himself as he remembered Pasquale remonstrating in the court room, while his lawyer tried to restrain him, and the judge beat with his gavel for order. 'What can an Afrikaaner know about capers and anchovy?' he had shouted. 'They are a people nurtured on *vetkoek* and *mampoer*! Kotze is the thief. How dare he claim this recipe! It's mine – composed in my own kitchen on the eve of Mandela's release from life-sentence. To hell with this imposter cook! Let him roast there for accusing me of taking his recipe!'

To protect Pasquale's life force from draining away, a plug had to be made. It was decided that this should be fashioned from human skin, a slice of human spleen (the organ of bitterness and revenge) and Pasquale's own hair. The first two components were easy to come by, since all types of body parts could be bought from the staff who loaded the incinerators at the hospital. They were not cheap, but they were clean and generally uncontaminated, and were delivered wrapped in cling-film within a day of ordering. Dambudzo would have to go to Pasquale's bedroom to procure the strands of his hair.

As he let himself in the back door of Da Pasquale, he heard Beatrice's sobbing voice, phoning someone from the bar; and saw to his horror the smashed statue on the floor. He made his way quietly upstairs, and felt nauseated by the smell and filth of the bedroom as he pulled the strands of hair from Pasquale's brush. Pasquale was not there and Dambudzo wondered where he was. He wanted to stay, to find out what had happened and to help Beatrice clean up the mess; but it was imperative that the plug be inserted without delay. All the signs in Pasquale's bedroom, and the smashed Virgin Mary in the kitchen confirmed that his demise was near. Gently tucking the hair into a pocket, Dambudzo crept out, unseen by Beatrice as she now crouched beside the shattered statue, crying.

Dr Baldinger rushed over as soon as Beatrice had phoned. He found her on the floor, crying tears which were old, and which had been buried deep within her since the day her mother had told her she was going. 'I'm just going to find someone, Baby,' she had said. 'And get a nice job and a nice house and then I'll fetch you. And I'll take you to a toy shop and you can choose any doll you want, because you'll be brave, waiting for me.'

Dr Baldinger lifted Beatrice and prised the pieces of china from her hands. He took a hanky from his pocket and gently wiped her face. With his arm around her shoulder, holding her to still her panic, he looked in dismay at the broken statue spread across the kitchen floor. Too aghast to speak, for he knew the statue's history and the trust with which it had been lent to Pasquale, he led Beatrice through to the bar, where he poured two glasses of port, and handed her one, saying, 'Drink it, drink it. Don't cry, my dear.'

He sipped slowly, pensively, and when Beatrice was calm and quiet he asked: 'Shall I call Primo? Should I walk you home now, Beatrice?'

Beatrice shook her head. 'I don't want him to know,' she replied.

'Well then, shall we just pick up the pieces, and tidy things a bit? Where is Pasquale?'

'In the pantry.'

'We'll leave him there a little, mmh?' He took off his coat and rolled up his sleeves. 'I'll just phone Alexia to tell her I'll be late.'

They spent the night picking up all the broken pieces, placing them on Pasquale's work surface, carefully assembling the different parts, and slowly recreating the broken form until the shards lay there like a large and difficult puzzle ready to be glued together. The splintered statue looked as a broken body might on a mortuary slab, awaiting forensic examination.

'Cloete is the man to help us,' said Doctor Baldinger. 'He did his internship at the military hospital. He's repaired many a body blown by grenades. But I can just imagine what he'll say to such a request.'

Cloete van Rensburg, although he had burst out laughing when Dr Baldinger phoned to ask him to reconstruct the statue, found the request rather charming and agreed to mend it. He arrived with tweezers, a surgical gown, his surgical loupes and tubes of superglue, and began the painstaking process of repair, watched by Dr Baldinger. His concentration was deep. His hands worked deftly and confidently. His posture hardly changed and he did not speak as he glued the pieces together.

183

It took him little more than an hour to repair the whole form and an hour to do the face alone, which he had left till last.

Dr Baldinger paced, as an expectant father might tread outside a delivery room. Beatrice sat at the pantry door, a headache pulsing at her temples. When all was quiet, and it was obvious Pasquale had fallen asleep, she went upstairs to clean the mess. Then she lay down and slept a shallow troubled sleep.

Finally Dr van Rensburg stepped back, stretched, took off his loupes and gown and asked for a cup of coffee. He pointed out to Dr Baldinger that the face would always show signs of its breakage. 'I see she's already had a minor repair – here, across the cheek,' he said. 'But with this new larger restoration, the eyes look more sorrowful than they probably did before. And look here at the mouth – the balance has been disturbed. She has lost the open, innocent look I imagine she once had. Her face now speaks of tribulation. Mind you, all reconstructed faces do. As you know, traumatic injuries to the flesh never happen neatly, and then the trauma lines dictate how the surgeon must work. You see the same here – the face shattered in three lines, so the hairline repair will always bear witness to the damage.'

'Her innocence has gone,' said Dr Baldinger.

'You could say so. But it probably went with the original old fracture. Where's Pasquale, by the way?'

'In the pantry,' replied Dr Baldinger. 'He locked himself in.'

'Has the love triangle finally imploded?' asked Cloete, laughing. 'Is that why he smashed the statue? Why don't you just leave him in the pantry, and call Primo to reclaim his wife? I know you're all friends but you must admit, Adam, the three of them are lunatics. Well, maybe not Beatrice, but her two men certainly are.'

'That's a bit harsh. Pasquale's just passionate – a bit volatile. He's worked up about problems in his kitchen. Lately he's been drinking more than usual. He was drunk when he broke the statue. And Primo, well, he's feeling depressed at the moment, understandably. I'm worried about him.

'We are indeed all good friends. So I won't pass judgement on what's happened.'

'No, I don't expect you to. I'm sorry if I sounded harsh. Now, if you'll excuse me, I won't stay to watch Pasquale exit the pantry. By the way, who shall I send my account to? Full reconstruction is not a cheap job – you know that!'

'Thanks for your help, Cloete. I really appreciate what you've done. Let me have your account,' said Dr Baldinger with a chuckle, placing the Virgin Mary back on her shelf, from where she again looked down at the kitchen.

'It'll be high,' said Cloete, grinning as he looked up at the statue. 'She's as close to perfect as I could possibly get her. So let's just say you owe me a good meal. Take me to the Brass Bell on a full moon. I like watching it over the sea.' He turned away. 'Right! I'm off!' he said, folding up his gown and packing his things. 'I'm operating at eleven. An ambassador is coming for a blepharoplasty. A man whose country is at war. How's that for vanity and cocked-up values?'

No one could persuade Pasquale to unlock the pantry – not Dr Baldinger, not Beatrice, and neither Mother Clementina nor Father Michael, who had come to see whether Pasquale was back at work, and were both shocked to hear that he had locked himself away. (Beatrice had led them through the kitchen to the pantry door and they had glanced up at the Virgin, both nodding to her in homage, neither noting through their myopia that her trusting and pure face had a new expression to it; nor that she was now laced in the fine lines of repair.)

All three implored Pasquale to come out, while Dr Baldinger went to look for a locksmith. In response Pasquale merely howled like a madman: 'What's happening? Beatrice! What's ruining my fruited bread? My innocent salami? I want to die, Beatrice! I can't live with this! It's driving me mad! Bring me my pistol!'

'Shouldn't you call the fire brigade, dear?' asked Mother Clementina.

'Yes,' agreed Father Michael. 'He could do himself

some damage in there. You do need to open up. You must get him out.'

'I think I'll call my husband,' replied Beatrice, fighting back tears and overwhelmed by a need to turn to Primo, to his calm bearing and steady, quiet love. 'He'll know what to do.'

Beatrice had never known Primo to do anything spiteful or malicious, and because he did not cast spells she did not suspect he had anything to do with Pasquale's predicament. She had not spoken to Primo since she had moved in with Pasquale, partly because she did not know how to approach him – she felt guilty, and strangely shy – but also because she did not want him to know how abusive Pasquale had become. There was an added factor: when he had phoned looking for her, and she had told him where she was, he had just hung up. She thought that by this action he was telling her not to come back.

Without knowing how she would ask for his help, she left Mother Clementina and Father Michael imploring at the pantry door and set off up Long and into Kloof Street. She walked up the familiar three steps of the stoep and, facing the two doors, unlocked 21A. As she crossed the threshold she felt herself brushing through spider webbing.

Primo was not home.

To Beatrice's astonishment, the once-locked room on the right, Eugenio's workshop, was wide open and all the timepieces were ticking. On the workbench, under the window, through which streamed the afternoon sunlight, was lined Primo's childhood collection of clocks. She touched his cuckoo clock and his little negro clock, smiling at the eyes which moved with the pendulum, and was suddenly flooded with memories of the day they had made friends. He had shown her and Pasquale a pedometer watch, then tied it to her leg and made her walk jerkily up and down the passage – up and down, up and down – until the watch dial had registered a hundred paces.

Beatrice now listened to the steady movements of the pendulums of the longcase clocks and remembered standing on a small bench to wind them, for this was Primo's task as a child, to wind his father's clocks and watches, and she was allowed to help.

Primo kept a record card monitoring the daily and monthly cycles of the various timepieces. They would wind them while Eugenio worked at his desk and Lidia cooked and baked or gardened. Pasquale would wait impatiently for them and complain. He declared the winding clocks a waste of time.

Beatrice walked down the passage. The house had a brightness to it, as though the roof was glass, and there was an unusual fragrance about, which she did not recognize. It was clear to her that Primo no longer lived alone, for she could see signs of someone else's influence – someone creative and sensitive; someone who enjoyed fresh flowers; who opened windows wide for breezes to tumble through; someone who liked order; someone young at heart, for there was gold glitter sprinkled about the house. Primo had taken in a lover, she concluded. How uncharacteristic of him, she thought, and how quickly this had happened. Beatrice felt a pang of jealousy.

She stopped at the other once-locked room, which was now also open. The window boarding had been removed and the contents dusted. As though an enchantment had been lifted, Primo's childhood room welcomed her and she wondered, looking in at its simple furnishings, who had convinced him to do this, when she had not succeeded.

Beatrice was in the kitchen when Primo and the Devil came in from their walk. Primo was overcome with emotion when he saw her. Thinking she had come back home, he took her in his arms and, barely keeping back tears, whispered his familiar endearment, 'Beata Beatrix'. Holding her tight to himself, feeling all his resentment lift, he ran his hands down her long hair and breathed in her presence. When he looked into her eyes he read, with disappointment, that she had not come home. She had merely come to ask for something. He was relieved that she had not seen Virginia, slumbering in his consulting room.

'What is it, Beata?' he asked softly, his heart pounding. He knew something was wrong. 'Tell me what's the matter,' he urged.

The Devil, invisible to Beatrice, reclined on the ottoman while Primo and his wife sat at the kitchen table. Beatrice struggled to ask for help for the man she assumed Primo must now hate. Primo took her hand. 'Tell me,' he said, and listened as she described the misfortune that had struck Pasquale and his subsequent breakdown. She said nothing of the violence that now raged through him.

'Please help me find out what's wrong. And help me get him out of the pantry, Primo. Will you come back with me? Will you break the door down? Will you talk to him?' she asked, and started to cry.

Primo recognized immediately that his malevolent spells had somehow activated and was stunned at the magnitude of their impact, and by the fact that they were also threatening Pasquale's physical and mental health. Though he was not a man who spoke untruths, nor one who excused or hid his actions, he did not tell Beatrice of his role in Pasquale's misfortune. Instead he looked across at the Devil, his friend, but was not sure what he read in those cabochon-jewelled eyes that held his gaze. He went through to the bedroom to fetch tissues. Seeing himself in the mirror, he noted deep sorrow in his eyes.

Returning, he said, 'Beata, I can tell you without hearing any more that this is bewitchment. Pasquale's breads and salami have a spell cast upon them. He won't be able to get himself out of this predicament. I'll have to do it for him.' Primo listened to himself speaking as soothsayer and magician. 'I'll work on it tonight, Beata. I'll look through my books. This isn't my field – bewitchment – you know that. But it's a small thing, I'm sure.' He averted his gaze from her. 'I won't need to speak to Pasquale. And I don't think it's appropriate for me to get him out of the pantry. You must call the fire brigade.'

They sat in silence. Primo felt himself the shy youth again, self-conscious and stumbling, unable to speak his heart. He was overwhelmed by feelings of anguish, wanting to break down, to ask: 'Why did you leave me, when you know I am nothing without you?' Instead, he took his wife's hand and asked, 'Beata, did I forget in our daily life to tell you that I love you?'

Beatrice, looking at his handsome, dignified countenance and only now properly facing the wrong she had done him, said, 'You did tell me, Primo. Every day and always.' She held back what her heart ached to say: But you too have someone else. There's someone new here, in my place.

'Beata,' he said. 'This will always be your home. You have your key. I'll never bolt the door from the inside.' He ran a hand under the gold chain which hung at her neck – a wedding gift to Beatrice from his father and aunt – studying the thick links and then looking into her eyes, remembering how his aunt had drawn its design on a piece of paper, for the jeweller Biccari to fashion. It was a copy of the chain Primo's grandmother had always worn, and which Lidia and Eugenio had handed over, along with their mother's ring and bracelets, when the Gestapo extorted fifty kilograms of gold from the Jews of Rome, falsely informing people that by paying it they would avoid deportation.

'I'd better go,' she said.

Primo walked her out to the stoep where they stood awkwardly for a moment.

'Primo,' she said, unexpectedly. 'Will you help me find Frankie?'

Beatrice had never asked Primo to trace her mother or find out what had happened to her. He had always known there would come a time when she would want to take this path, to search, to uncover locked secrets, but he chose not to prompt her in that direction, knowing it would only bring pain. He wondered, now, what had stirred in her to make her want to open the closed trinket box in which she had hidden away her childhood yearnings for the mother who had left her in the care of others.

'You will hurt yourself, Beata. But, yes, we can look for her, if you want.'

'I do,' she said. 'I've never wanted to find her. But now I do. I want to know why she never came back to fetch me.'

Primo held Beatrice and kissed her lips, lightly. She said goodbye and he repeated, 'This is your home, Beata.'

A trail of fire ran through him. He wanted to take his wife inside, undress her, reclaim the territory of her body, which he felt was rightly his. Instead he quelled his desire, and watched her until she reached the traffic lights, then came indoors and stood before the Pre-Raphaelite painting in the lounge. He touched its lips and then his own. 'Beata Beatrix,' he whispered. 'I love you.'

'I should wake your client now,' said the Devil, standing in the doorway, watching him. 'It will soon be dark. She ought to go home.'

On her way home, Beatrice stopped outside Sissy-and-Esquire and asked Meduro whether he could break down the pantry door. Meduro, leaning against the shop window, wore a white shirt tied in a knot at his waist, the buttons all undone, the peppercorn hair of his chest forming a small path towards his navel. Tight denims accentuated his strong thighs. His sunglasses were perched on his head.

'Sure,' he said. 'It is no problem. I just tell Miss Sissy where I be.'

He arrived at Da Pasquale with a sledgehammer and asked Dr Baldinger and the locksmith to give him space. With two blows he knocked the door open. Pasquale lay in the furthest corner, naked, his body in a foetal position, his arms wrapped tightly around a ten-kilogram can of imported tomato concentrate. His skin was clammy and his hair drenched in sweat.

Meduro carried the limp Pasquale upstairs and helped Beatrice wash him. They oiled him with lavender and dressed him in his pyjamas before tucking him under the feather eiderdown. Then they stepped back so Dr Baldinger could examine him.

That night Meduro said to Sissy, 'Such a one, such a one as Mr Pasquale, in Congo, we leave him to die. Such a one who is so thin, so mad – for what purpose is there to help such a one to live?'

Sissy laughed. 'You say he's mad, Medu? He's lost it completely? That's funny. He's always seen himself as the great lover-boy of Long Street. So what's happened? He has a little affair with that air-head Beatrice and bang go his senses.' She shook her head. 'I tell you, the next one to go mad will be his sister. When she finds out Cloete comes here, she'll also throw a fit or two.'

They were sitting on the carpet at the foot of the bed, playing bao and drinking rum. She had on a transparent white gown. He wore a cloth around his loins. Esquire sat between them, staring at the mahogany seeds of the game. Scented candles gave a tranquil light to the bedroom.

'You like your friend Virgin?' asked Meduro.

'Virginia? God, she's no more virgin than I am, Medu. You must get people's names right. "Contessa" is how she likes to be known.' Sissy paused. 'Sometimes I like her. Sometimes I like her around. Not all the time. Sometimes for coffee and to find out what's going on with everybody. She knows everyone's business and I like to know too. And she buys a lot from me, you know that. Now she also wants a little scar pattern across her body. She'll come in soon for that.'

'I do a good job for her. You know what pattern she want?'

'No,' said Sissy, refilling their glasses. 'Something tribal, I think. You help her decide.' She smiled. 'I like more to play with her man – with Cloete – more than with her. Do you mind when I play with Cloete, Medu?'

'I mind, yes,' he said. 'Dr Cloete not my friend.'

'Actually, he's not mine either, Medu.'

She untied her belt and shrugged so her gown fell off her shoulders. 'Come, Medu. Come kiss Maman, come make love to me. When he comes tonight, I won't answer the door.'

Meduro moved the bao board aside and crawled over to her. He took off his loincloth and knotted it around his head. Then, with a gentleness which belied his strong physique, he pushed her backwards so she lay on the carpet. He kissed the flatness between her breasts as his hands began to caress her body, preparing it to receive his. Esquire arched his back and sat close to them, watching.

Sissy did not tell Meduro that at times when she and Virginia had lain together, in the top-floor room of the Stairway to Paradise, their women's bodies had touched each other with a skin-to-skin softness not unlike that of mist touching fine *fynbos*; that Virginia's tongue, exploring her body, had aroused her quite as much as any man had ever done; that this had been as close to love as she had ever come. Though she loved no one.

Even though Primo tried, working through the night and consulting his many volumes on magic and sorcery, he could not reverse the bad spells and energies he had set. Fuelling themselves with self-generating meanness and spite, the spells had mutated a hundredfold, forming interlocking barbs of malice. He realized that only a magician experienced in the structuring of evil would have had the skill to disempower them, and even he, not having cast the spells himself, might have had difficulty. Primo had to ask the Devil for help.

The Devil reminded Primo that he was not versed in the construction of evil. 'Evil is not my work,' he said. 'But let me try to unravel your spells. I imagine them to be like an entanglement – a disorderliness of energy that we would have to undo and straighten out.'

While the Devil worked in the garden, under the mulberry tree, Primo lay on the ottoman, emotionally exhausted by Beatrice's visit and his futile attempts at negating the spells. He was grateful for the Devil's help, given so willingly and without question, and reflected on this kindness, wondering how he would have managed had he been alone.

The Devil untangled the spells as though they were a mass of entwined embroidery cottons, following each line of wizardry into the centre, combing them, unknotting and diffusing their malignancies. It took him the whole afternoon. When he had finished he left the house and went out on his own.

Dr Baldinger was puzzled by Pasquale's presenting symptoms of fever, derangement and muscle wastage, for there was no evidence of bacterial or viral infection, nor of parasitic infestation. He paced up and down, his black coat swirling as he turned on his heel at each end of the room.

'If I didn't know better, I'd say there was bewitchment here,' he muttered. Then he turned to Beatrice and said, 'Though I am reminded of his old breakdowns. I thought he was well recovered from all that.'

Finally he simply recorded Pasquale as suffering dehydration and anxiety. He set up a drip and sedated Pasquale, who slept deeply for the next twenty-four hours. In this time he did not toss or turn and seemed to be spared dreams and nightmares. Once or twice he opened his dark eyes and stared into the distance.

*   *   *

While Pasquale slept, Primo came to complete the Devil's work by realigning towards good the energies of the delicatessen and the apartment. On the landing he noticed a basket full of Pasquale's shoes, and realized he had not told the Devil about the shoelace spell. Well, he thought to himself, he wouldn't bother the Devil with this; perhaps at a later stage he would tackle the enchantment himself; for the moment he was sure Pasquale could live with it. He found entering the bedroom of his wife's lover distasteful, though he kept jealousy at bay. Even so, the sight of Pasquale's pale and death-like form disturbed him, and he felt remorse for having caused his near-demise. He embraced Beatrice and greeted Dr Baldinger and Father Michael with a nod.

'Good to see you, Primo. How are you? What do you make of this?' asked Dr Baldinger. 'Some bewitchment here, perhaps?'

'I make nothing of it,' answered Primo, bluntly.

'Ah, Mr Verona, how nice to see you again!' exclaimed Father Michael. 'How grateful I still am to you for helping us locate Sister Mary Agnes when she went missing.'

He turned to Dr Baldinger and said, 'Poor dear, she quite forgot she was a nun. At the age of seventy-five she told the security guard she was going home and walked out of the front gate, brazen as you please! We hunted high and low for her. We all imagined the worst, of course. It was Mr

Verona here who found her for us, with the help of his marvellous crystal ball. You'll never guess where! Gambling at the new casino out in Goodwood!'

Dr Baldinger smiled. Everyone knew the story of Sister Mary Agnes and how she had crept into the geriatric section of Nazareth House, taken a set of clothes from one of the residents, filled an overnight bag with brass candlesticks from the chapel and then asked a *bergie* to pawn them for her.

'Where is the good sister now?' he asked, well knowing that she had gone to live in Brooklyn with a group of orphans she had once cared for, now grown and into all sorts of illegal rackets and schemes. She had turned her back on her past pious and holy ways and set herself on a gambling trajectory, amassing a small fortune, then losing it all.

'Ah, she's back in Ireland. Retired now and in care. Back in the home country,' replied Father Michael.

Dr Baldinger turned to Beatrice and, clicking his bag shut, said, 'Beatrice, you need to strengthen him up. Good chicken soup, made with giblets and lots of root vegetables, will do it. And give him beetroot tonic. Old-fashioned remedies these may be, but they'll get him back on his feet.'

He and Primo walked out together. 'Primo,' asked the Doctor, 'how've you been?'

'I'm well, under the circumstances,' said Primo.

'Then don't make yourself so scarce. I miss our friendship. Answer your door sometimes.'

Primo said nothing. He just bowed slightly in farewell, and walked away. Dr Baldinger, saddened and more concerned than ever, watched his friend make his way up Long Street.

Late that night Lovemore slipped quietly into Pasquale's bedroom, lay on his back and slid under the bed, where he tied onto one of the wooden slats the small bundle of magic components wrapped in a piece of hessian and bound tightly with string. It was no larger than a man's middle finger. He was so quiet that he did not disturb Beatrice as she lay fast asleep at Pasquale's side.

When Pasquale woke up the next evening, the memory of what had happened hovered over him as the remains of a nightmare might, and he had little recollection of the details of his ordeal. He sensed he had suffered a debilitating sickness, and that he had come close to death. Dr Baldinger described his condition only as malaise, and Pasquale was content not to pursue the matter.

Da Pasquale reopened soon after the enchantment that plagued the fruited breads and salami had lifted. It was a Saturday and the southeast wind had cast a cloth of cloud across Table Mountain. Pasquale saw this as a good omen, believing it symbolized one of his own tables, spread out in generosity and warm hospitality. His return to the kitchen was prodigal. He was welcomed tenderly and with broad smiles by Lovemore and Dambudzo – wearing the white starched aprons of their trade – who felt confident of his new wellness and secure in the strength of the counter-magic they had composed. (Their supplier had informed them that the slither of spleen had belonged to a magistrate, that it had been acquired on the very morning of delivery, and that the character of its previous host would ensure success. The small length of skin had been retrieved from Dr van Rensburg's surgical-waste bin.)

From his newly provisioned storage drums Pasquale took stone-ground Wuppertaal flour, which he mixed with equal quantities of ground almonds. In a separate bowl he prepared a fondant paste of crushed hazelnuts and rose-water, working into it orange rind and pulverized roasted fig. To these he added his liquids, yeast, spices, sultanas and cherries. Combining everything, he worked up a large marbled dough and allowed it to rise before shaping it into individual loaves. While these baked, Lovemore and Dambudzo waited outside in the sun and Pasquale sat watching the glass door of the oven, his heartbeat accelerated and clamminess coating his body. But there was no need for him to be concerned – the first batch of fruited breads lifted from the oven was perfect. Dambudzo placed them in a row on a cooling rack and, while they were still warm, helped Pasquale pour on a topping of ground caramelized almonds. Then they all went to drink at the bar, Pasquale drained of energy, his waiters glowing with pride.

Mother Clementina and Father Michael came to visit late that afternoon.

'We've decided, the other sisters and I, and Father Michael here, to let our statue stay with you indefinitely – my, this is delicious, dear, thank you,' said Mother Clementina, sipping from the sangria Beatrice had poured her.

'Yes,' agreed Father Michael. 'This is most refreshing – nice and fruity. As we were saying . . . yes, our statue has certainly brought an air of benevolence and beneficence to your kitchen, we all agree on that.'

'If you will allow her to continue to oversee your kitchen and good work,' said Mother Clementina, 'we would be delighted to leave her with you. And we feel certain that old Mr Biccari would not object at all.'

Pasquale led them through to the kitchen and they looked up at the statue. He did not remember smashing her and no one had told him of his drunken deed. The Virgin Mary's look had changed, he thought now, but he could not quite work out what was different about her. 'She has aged with me,' he said.

'Oh, Mr Benvenuto, she is ageless. Time does not

touch her, nor line her face,' said Father Michael. 'Now, let us not keep you from your work. Good day. Let me just add how pleased we are to see you well.'

Pasquale decided to wait a few months before curing any salami, for he was still weak and tired easily, but Beatrice and all his friends felt confident that life had, by some miracle, almost returned to normal.

That first Saturday night of reopening, Da Pasquale was full, with every table occupied and all space at the bar taken. Pasquale offered only a simple seafood risotto with bean and fennel salad, cheeses and breads; and of course the fruited breads with dessert wine. Friends and customers came in, shook Pasquale's hand, embraced him, commended his recovery (though he still looked wan), wished him back his strong stature and lifted their glasses to good life and health. Lazar played his violin and mellowness settled over everyone. Lovemore and Dambudzo could hardly cope, for no one had thought to advertise for casual waiters.

Before the card players took their places at the window table, Pasquale led Biccari through to his kitchen, to show him the statue of the Virgin Mary. 'Do you know this is from your father, Biccari?' he asked. 'No? Come sit and I'll tell you a piece of your history while you play cards. But I'll say this first:

that it is only since Mother Clementina lent her to me that I am well. She is a statue of miracles. Beatrice will pour us all another round of drinks, to honour your father's memory.'

'We should throw a party for you, Pasqui,' suggested Sack, putting his arm round his friend. 'To celebrate. We thought we'd lost you there for a moment.'

'That's an excellent idea,' said Stern. 'We need to liven up a bit – now that we're out of the doldrums.'

'How does a street party sound?' suggested Bregman. 'We could close off Long Street, bring in music. What do you think, Romana?'

'That would be wonderful. We haven't had a party for so long. It's time already.'

'We should all wear masks,' said Virginia, who was sitting at the bar, drinking vodka on ice. 'I think it should be a masked party, a masked fancy-dress, to give some sense of artistry to the occasion.' She lit a cigarette and drew deeply.

'A masked party, yes,' said Sack. 'We can create a Venetian carnival right here in Long Street.'

'Let everyone know. Invite everyone,' said Solomon, shuffling a pack and handing it to Emerich.

'Yes,' agreed Dr Baldinger. 'Invite Primo too, and someone make sure he comes. It's time he came back to us. He's locked himself away for long enough now. I miss our debates. I need some philosophical challenge.'

'You know,' said Emerich, pausing as he dealt the

cards, 'I saw him out walking the other evening, wearing a long robe, the kind Orthodox priests wear, talking to himself with great animation. He needs our company.'

'Yes,' agreed Biccari. 'But now tell us, Pasqui, this story about my father and your statue.'

Beatrice looked away. She wanted to go home to Primo, to thank him, to say sorry, to explain, to repair the three-cornered friendship, to undo some of the hurt. But when she had mentioned this to Pasquale, he had started to cry. They were the tears of a broken man and they disarmed her. She had lain with him, stroking his wet face, stilling his agitation.

She would look out for Primo at the party, she decided, and to make sure that he came she would phone Dr Baldinger the next day to say she would deliver an invitation herself.

Virginia brought Beatrice's thoughts back to the bar by knocking her empty glass against it, saying, 'I'm not going to stay long, Beatrice. Just give me another double to celebrate my brother's good health. The Stairway's busy tonight. We've had a busload of Japanese tourists book the place for the whole weekend.' She crushed her cigarette stub into the ashtray and lit another. Her hands trembled.

That morning Cloete had unlocked his surgery to find her waiting for him, brandishing his breast-reduction scissors and a scalpel. 'You're also a bastard!' she had growled between clenched teeth as she made a strike at his face. A thin line of blood beaded across his cheek. He caught her arms and prised the instruments from her hands, throwing them across the room, then forcing her down onto the couch.

Virginia began to cry, saying, 'I know what's going on. You can't fool me. You're a liar and a cheat, aren't you? Who are you two-timing me with? Is it someone I know?'

Cloete kissed her lips, smarting at the stale taste of brandy and nicotine. 'No one,' he said. 'I have one angel and that's you. Now, give me back my key and let's just talk, shall we? We'll make a little love here like we used to and then just talk sensibly, like two adults. You used to like that, remember? Love in my examination room?' He unzipped her black dress and pulled it down. She was naked underneath. Across her breasts marched a newly incised line of tribal markings – single vertical cuts – the scabs just dry. Cloete turned away in disgust, wiping his cheek against his sleeve.

As he locked the door of his office, so they would not be disturbed, he realized the time had come to end their relationship. It had entered unnavigable waters and he was no seaman.

The Devil handed Primo a card. 'Someone slipped this under the door,' he said.

It was an invitation to a masked party to be held in celebration of Pasquale's recovery and the reopening of his delicatessen. The party, it said, was to be held in Long Street on the following Saturday night. Primo tossed the card onto the table. The Devil picked it up and read it.

'You ought to go,' he said, responding to Primo's lack of interest. 'You should reintegrate. This might be a good way of doing it.'

Primo looked across the table at his friend, at this angel who had come into his life at its lowest point and comforted him. He did not want the company of others, did not need others to love him or give him a sense of relevance. He was content to live with the Devil.

'Why should I reintegrate when I have you?' he asked. 'I no longer have need for people. I actually enjoy seclusion. I would like only my wife back. Only Beatrice.'

A sudden fear came over Primo – that the Devil too would abandon him. 'Are you thinking of leaving me, Lucifer?' he asked. 'Is that why you want me to reintegrate – so that you can go back to the Afterlife, back to your own world?' You must never leave, he thought. You must stay here, with me, where there is no fire.

The Devil flexed his wings. A shimmering of fine gold dust whirled through the shaft of sunlight coming through the kitchen door. He did not answer Primo's questions. He said simply, 'It will be good for you to go to the party. It would not be wise to cut yourself off for too long.

'I am sure your wife will be there. It might be the right time to make things good again. Would it help if I go with you? I can stay at your side.'

Neither spoke for a moment. Then Primo said, 'Yes, I'll go to the masked party if you come with me. But I want you to be visible. I want you to show yourself to everyone, to be seen as my friend. I would go if you came openly as my companion, so I am not seen to be alone as a discarded husband or an abused friend.'

The Devil, pondering Primo's request, turned to look out of the door, at the rosemary bushes crowned with blue flowers. At length he said, 'This is a difficult request you make. It would not be a safe thing for me to do. I would put myself in great peril. For, in order to be fully visible – to others, that is, to those who are not clairvoyant as you are – I would have to incarnate, be made flesh. I could become trapped. As angels, we are discouraged from taking material form. If something should happen, if something prevented us from leaving the confines of flesh, our angelic energies could for ever become ensnared.'

'No harm will come to you,' said Primo. 'We'll be in Long Street and I know it well. The clubs will remind you of the Underworld – the gambling, the smoking, the idling of time. It must all be the same, here and Hell. You'll feel at home.' They sat silently for a moment. Then Primo said, 'I need you, Lucifer.'

'You tempt me,' responded the Devil.

'Yes,' agreed Primo. 'I tempt you. Come with me.'

'Will you be mindful of me?'

'I'll be mindful, Lucifer. I'll watch over you. I'll not allow any harm to come to you.'

'Who will we say I am?' asked the Devil.

'No one will ask. We'll all be costumed and masked, of course,' replied Primo.

'How shall we costume ourselves?' asked the Devil.

'As devils!' Primo laughed. 'Let's go as devils!'

Primo reclaimed Long Street as his own on the day he bought two black suits, one for himself and one for the Devil, from Sissy-and-Esquire, and carried them home, beautifully wrapped in tissue and tied up in a box. Sissy Plumb had asked him why he wanted *two* dress suits, in exactly the same trouser size but one with an extra-large coat instead of a jacket, and both with red silk lapel-roses. He refused to tell her, even when she probed as she wrapped his purchases.

'So, you have a twin brother, Primo, one that you've never told us about? You bugger – what other secrets have you got?' She sucked on her cigarette holder, held in the smoke, then blew it above him. 'Tell me, what's the occasion? Is there a wedding coming up that I haven't been invited to? A bar mitzvah? Or is it the masked party? Don't tell me you're coming to that, Primo! I know you hate raving it up. By the way, have you got over your jilted-husband complex? Won't you mind seeing Beatrice at the party with her lover-boy, hey? Be honest, now.'

He said nothing, so Sissy tried another tack. 'Well, you've gone your whole life wearing those tired linen suits of yours and now you're busting out and buying two new ones! What's got into you?'

Primo thought Sissy a fool at the best of times, and had never engaged in conversation with her. Even when she asked bluntly, peering over her diamanté sunglasses, '*Who* are you taking with you to the masked ball? Who have you dragged out of the woodwork? You can tell me – I won't spill your little secret,' he merely smiled.

It was late in the day. The traffic was heavy with commuters leaving the city centre. As Primo strolled down the pavement, glancing in at Da Pasquale, at Maginty's, at Stairway to Paradise, his carriage was upright and his step brisk. He found he was singing to himself. His heart had brightness in it.

The setting sun lent a particular light to the evening, so that all colours seemed polished. Primo wondered, as he climbed the steps of his stoep, how it was that he had never properly remarked the scarlet of the geraniums or the purple of the pelargoniums filling the planters and pots cluttering the veranda. He looked up at the sky – which was cut through with streaks of cloud – and realized, with great satisfaction, that he was happy.

* * *

rimo unlocked the door and walked in as his father's clocks began the noisy business of striking six o'clock, in welcome, he thought. 'Lucifer!' he shouted. 'I'm home!'

He put the box on his bed, untied the strings and took off the lid. From the top drawer of Beatrice's dressing table he lifted out all her underwear, stuffed the fuss of silks and satins into the second drawer and crammed it shut.

Into the drawer he carefully placed, side by side, two new shirts, two cummerbunds, two bow ties and two crimson lapel-roses. He hung the suits, which Sissy had sprayed lightly with lemon grass, in the wardrobe, among Beatrice's dresses. He had bought two devil masks from Golden Dragon Gifts in the Malay quarter. These he placed on the dressing table.

Primo went to the kitchen and put on the coffee. On the table stood a bowl of fuchsias and a box of delicacies from Da Pasquale, left on his stoep that morning by Dr Baldinger and brought in by the Devil. The windows and back doors were open and the evening air tumbled in, swirling round the fresh flowers, lifting their fragrances and diffusing them about the house. In the back courtyard, the Devil was repotting the violets.

Primo opened the Da Pasquale box. Why not? he thought as he ate a *polpetta* and then a second, still warm, and noting from their delicious piquancy that Pasquale was back on form. Taking his coffee outside he greeted the Devil and sat down on a chair under the tree. As he watched the Devil at work he realized that he loved looking at him. There was an air of great beauty and effortless serenity about him all the time. His face was youthful and unlined, yet wise with age.

Today he was wearing a white vestment that seemed to have been made from a single piece of cloth, for there were no seams at the sleeves. Instead there were many tiny pleats running down from the neck, giving the impression that the garment could be opened out, like a fan.

The Devil wore a different robe every day, though he had brought no luggage. Primo had put a duvet and pillow down on the ottoman, but there were never signs that the Devil slept. Did he go home each night to change? Primo wondered. It seemed intrusive to ask. Perhaps he slept sitting up; maybe his wings were bothersome.

The Devil stepped back from the violets and, with a look of satisfaction, took off his gardening gloves and asked Primo to help him carry in the pots. Together they lined them up along both kitchen window ledges.

'We have wonderful gardens in Hell,' remarked the Devil, dusting the leaves of the violets. 'We mirror the gardens of earth, and the seasons. Some are laid out with beautiful walkways and fountains and recesses where souls can sit to ponder. Others we leave wild, to seed themselves and follow their own designs. In spring the whole of Hell is heady with fragrance.' He paused. 'I speak of the Underworld, of course. Nothing grows in Deep Hell.' He paused again. 'Well, that is not entirely true. There is a garden there. It is a paper garden, a garden of flowers folded from papyrus and linen paper. And it is quite beautiful, for the flowers are exquisitely made. They are not brightly coloured, but have the natural tones of the papers we use: whites and creams and buffs. They are laid out in formal gardens, like works of art, and there is a stillness because there are no bees or butterflies. Nor is there any fragrance to speak of.' He smiled. 'You are wondering who folds the flowers?' he asked, reading the question in Primo's eyes. 'They are made by those in the Underworld who do not play cards.'

He sat down at the kitchen table and asked, 'Have you bought our suits?'

'I have,' answered Primo. 'We're going to be a sensation.'

'Indeed,' replied the Devil, with a twinkle in his eye. After a pause he asked, 'Would you like me to show you how to fold a marsh lily? Do you have any papyrus or linen paper? Even crêpe paper will do.'

*   *   *

n the night of the masked party Primo reflected, as he stepped out of the shower, on the perils of incarnation that the Devil had mentioned. What could trap Lucifer? If he became caught in his incarnation, would the entrapment be perpetual? Would Lucifer remain angelic within the human form, or would his energy devolve to a human one? If so, once the human form he had taken had died, would he revert to his angelic state? Did other angels incarnate at times and unwittingly become trapped? Are there angels here among us? Are there angels on earth?

These were Primo's thoughts as he shaved, then brushed his thick curls. He was pleased with the reflection that looked back from the mirror. There was strength in his eyes. The expression lines on his face spoke not of anguish but of a journey, as a map would. There were none he wished to erase.

He went through to the bedroom where the Devil, wearing only black trousers, held out the dress shirt. The sight of him startled Primo. His torso – ivory white, smooth and hairless – seemed to have been cut from marble. His immense wings, at rest, had a sheen to them that glistened in the light of the room, as did the thick mahogany curls that rested on his broad naked shoulders. Primo's eyes traced the form of the Devil's upper body: the strong neck, the lines of his pectoral musculature, the firm biceps and triceps, his large hands – all of which spoke of great physical strength. Are you a man? Primo wanted to ask. Pure man? First man? Made by the direct breath of God? Unspoilt by evil?

Seeming to read his thoughts, the Devil spread his wings, then brought them to rest against his back again, as if to say: I am no man. I am an angel.

'I can't put the shirt on,' said the Devil. 'There are no openings for my wings.'

Primo took the shirt and, with a pocketknife, cut two long slits down the back of it. He helped ease the Devil's folded wings through them. He lent him a pair of socks and black shoes. He stilled an urge to take the Devil in his arms, to caress the wings.

'I'll help you with your coat,' Primo offered.

The Devil's wings lay against his back. Primo held them down with the cummerbund and helped the Devil put one arm, then the other, through the tailcoat sleeves. He turned the collar down and ran his palms over the hump formed by the wings, flattening creases and making sure no feathers were visible. The Devil turned and they faced each other as Primo pinned a red silk rose to the Devil's lapel and then one to his own. They clipped on their bow ties. Then they stood before the long mirror of the wardrobe door. The Devil's mahogany curls and Primo's black curls, streaked with grey, tumbled to their shoulders. They looked like brothers, though one stood upright and the other had a disfiguring hump on his back.

If the Devil was still apprehensive about incarnating, he did not say so.

For the party, Long Street was closed to traffic between Bloem Street and the Buitensingel intersection. Tables and chairs were set out on the pavements outside cafés and restaurants. Streamers and balloons waved in the breeze.

Although it had been billed to start at nine o'clock, the hour at which night would darken the long summer day, by seven the road was already a crush of party energy fuelled by music, drugs and drink. Smells of hot chips, popcorn, fish sizzling on *skottel braais*, garlic rolls, fried onion and *boerewors* mingled with the heady aftershaves, perfumes and perspiration of the milling crowd.

As darkness fell, the streetlights were turned off and fairy lights, draped across balconies and shop-fronts, were switched on. They twinkled and, with the subdued lighting of cafés and restaurants, gave a gentle and romantic touch to the street.

Vendors sold *bunnychows, sosaties* and *salomies*. Stands offered spiced wine in paper cups. Tequila shots were on sale at several corners. Dealers selling cocaine, Ecstasy and Mandrax were out in force, some strolling up and down, others doing their business outside Bregman's Afrika and Emerich's Bliss. Hookers leant up against walls or stood in-vitingly outside clubs.

The area between Pepper Street and Orphan Lane was reserved for dancing. Here the Billy Monk Jazz Band from Manenberg and Lazar alternated, giving time to tango lovers, rockers and *langarm* dancers alike.

Restaurateurs struggled to cope with the demand for food and drink, every table being taken. There were queues. Most pavement stalls sold out long before the night was over.

A mixed crowd of wealthy locals, tourists, backpackers, dancers and *kwerekwere* jostled and swayed, hungry for sensation and pleasure. Drunks, bums and street children wormed their way through the revellers, scoring scraps of food or picking pockets and handbags. Though the body of the crowd moved and pulsed, squirmed and danced, its masked faces were expressionless.

Many of the masks were simple, full face in black or white. Others were elaborate with attached hairpieces. There were character masks among them too: Goldilocks, Marilyn Monroe, Nefertiti and Cleopatra. A pig and a sun god sipped vodka from straws.

A group wearing Venetian masks lounged outside the recently reopened Da Pasquale. Around the white-clothed tables, drinking wine, sat Pulcinella, Pantalone, the Plague Doctor and a number of figures wearing classic white masks. Inside, the poker players, in their tell-tale black suits and wearing white half-face masks, concentrated on their cards and gave little attention to the surrounding revelry. Dr Baldinger – wearing a white surgical mask and identifiable by his black trench coat – watched them play.

At a nearby table, costumed in a black suit and tie, a wig of knotted hair and a white full-faced mask, sat the Hunchback of Notre Dame, alone. This figure was tall, drank a lot and did not revel or laugh.

Because Pasquale still tired easily, he closed shop at eleven. The card players moved on to Maginty's Cigar Bar and resumed their game at a centre table. Untroubled by the loud music and tightly packed patrons, they drank and continued to challenge their luck and skills. Dr Baldinger, having walked Alexia home, returned to their company.

Lovemore and Dambudzo stayed on at Da Pasquale to eat supper and drink a beer before going home. They did not join the party. Pasquale bid them goodnight from the foot of the stairs, and they watched him make his weary way up. He was too weak to make love, too tired to hold Beatrice. 'I feel so feeble. I'm still so weary from that illness. You go back to the party if you want.'

'No, I'll stay with you. It sounds rowdy now.' She touched his cheek. 'You didn't eat anything, Pasqui. Aren't you hungry? Maybe that's why you feel weak. Can I bring you something? Some toast and black tea?'

'No, nothing. I'm not hungry. I'm glad you've come up with me. Don't put out the light. Stay here, stay with me. Don't leave me, Beatrice.'

Beatrice tucked him up and dimmed the lights, then went out onto the balcony. She sat looking down at the street party below, wondering whether Primo had come, and with whom, and sorry she had not seen him.

Dambudzo and Lovemore washed their plates and, as Dambudzo switched the lights off, he looked up at the statue of the Virgin Mary. Her eyes seemed troubled. Walking away from Long Street towards the station, he said, 'Mr Pasquale broke the Holy Mother. I saw her smashed on the floor. But he was quick to fix her up again. He fixed her up before everyone saw her broken. But I saw her broken.'

'He smashed the Holy Mother?' asked Lovemore in disbelief, crossing himself. 'We must put something down for her. We must give her offerings. Or more trouble will surely come.'

His thoughts turned to the days when he served as an altar boy at the Italian Chapel in Masvingo; and how once a snake had slithered in to find cool from the dry harsh heat of midday, only to be beaten to death with a knobkerrie by the priest, who then ordered the young Lovemore to take the carcass out; and how he had placed it behind the graves of the Italian prisoners of war who had died so far from their homes, their hearts broken by exile. Some of the snake's body fluids had splashed against a mural of the Virgin Mary, wetting her carefully painted garment. Lovemore had wiped the robe clean with the edge of his shirt, fearing a bad omen, for he knew well that the Devil had entered Eden garbed as a snake. He recited the Hail Mary five times but, even so, that night *magandanga* – guerrilla soldiers – had entered a nearby kraal looking for sell-outs. To make an example, to warn people not to give support to Ian Smith's army, they had burnt a whole family to death inside a hut, first tying their hands behind their backs with wire.

'The Holy Mother likes the white lilies. This much I know. We must put white lilies for her tomorrow,' he said, as they boarded their train to Woodstock.

Meanwhile, Primo and the Devil walked up and down Long Street, each attired in his new suit and wearing a horned mask that completely covered his face. They cut identical figures and had the same way of walking: tall and confident, each with one hand in a pocket. Except the Devil had a hump on his back. So there were two hunchbacks in the crowd that night.

recognize everything; yes, this is so like the Underworld,' said the Devil. 'Except for the children. There are no children in Hell. But the jazz bands, the roistering, it is just like a reflection. This is obviously why the newly dead have no trouble adjusting. It must all be the same for them, superficially.'

Two hookers fell into step with them. One pressed herself against Primo, took his hand and held it to her breast. He pushed her away. The other linked arms with the Devil and offered him quick sex in the alley for a hundred rand.

As the night progressed, people with the means and the mind to left the street and headed for the clubs and bars. The outdoor musicians packed up and went home. Disco music now throbbed. The street crowd, meanwhile, had become an animal of one body, one drunken spirit, swollen with those drawn by the music from all over the city, heaving up and down Long Street. The edges tattered as people peeled away to drink, to urinate against walls, to vomit cocktails of alcohol and drugs. Some fell and were trampled. Men's hands pulled at girls' skimpy tops, grabbed at breasts, pinched thighs. Women shrilled in protest. Pressed against shopfronts, couples kissed and caressed; some fornicated in alleys, driving their passions with fury into each other's bodies. There was foulness in the late night air.

'Let's go inside now,' suggested Primo, and he led the Devil into Maginty's, where they made their way to the bar. Primo ordered a glass of tomato juice.

Across the room, Harlequin, with Snow White perched on his knee and nibbling at his neck, sat at a corner table. He noticed the two figures in black at the bar, masked as devils. One leaned over the counter, to pay the barman. The other, a hunched figure, looked around at the people in the club. This second figure turned in Harlequin's direction. The clasp of his devil mask came undone and the mask fell, revealing a face of extraordinary beauty.

Harlequin, immediately struck by the beauty of the man looking towards him, removed his own mask, to better see the face of the hunchback, and so revealing his identity: Cloete van Rensburg. He asked Snow White if she knew who the hunched newcomer was.

'That's Primo's gay-boy,' Snow White told him. 'You'd think he'd score better than a humpback.'

'Are you sure?' asked Cloete, staring across at the stranger.

'Of course I'm sure,' she replied. 'That's Primo with him. I sold them those suits. I measured them up myself. Armani. Expensive. Primo paid for both. The lover's a bum.' She took off her mask and laughed. 'Hey, man! Primo finally read his own crystal ball and found out he's a *moffie*. Good on Beatrice.' She stood up. 'Hey, everyone! Primo's climbed out of the wardrobe at last!' she shrilled above the din of drinkers.

Cloete elbowed his way through the crowd and stood before the unmasked stranger. Sissy followed.

Even though he had been drinking heavily, Cloete's senses realigned themselves enough to realize that here was the most beautiful living face he had ever seen: the face of perfection, the *Testa di Adamo* released from its deft lines and given living form. His thoughts fumbled to find a word to describe the face. All he could come up with was 'angelic'. He did not need his measuring calipers to verify the symmetrical alignment of its features, the equipoise between brow and jaw, the correspondence between the orbital cavities, the balance between lips and nose. The rush of emotions that seized him – elation, disbelief, wonder – curdled under the influence of alcohol and expressed themselves aggressively. He grabbed at Primo's arm. 'Who is your friend, Primo?' he demanded. 'Introduce me to him!'

Primo pulled back his arm and knocked over his tomato juice. Red spread across the counter.

'Who are you?' demanded Cloete breathlessly, leaning close to the Devil's face.

'I am Lucifer,' replied the Devil.

'Lucifer!' shrilled Sissy. 'How hard-core can you get? Hell, Primo! You've found yourself some kinky stuff here – a hunchback called Lucifer. Why've you kept him all to yourself, you old chop?'

Primo did not want to engage with either Cloete or Sissy. Sissy would draw unwanted attention and Cloete's uncharacteristic aggression alarmed him. He took off his mask and indicated to the Devil that they should go. The Devil nodded, but as he turned away from Cloete and Sissy, Cloete grabbed at his coat and shouted, 'No! Don't go! I have to speak to you! Where do you come from? Who are you?'

Primo pushed Cloete hard and out of the way so he fell against the bar. A ripple of agitation ran through the club, as though a challenge had been thrown down and now the drinkers, through a blur of alcohol, were weighing up how to respond. Primo and the Devil shoved a way through the packed bar and out into the street crowd, then tried to edge their way along the pavement.

The outside crowd had more than doubled. Primo felt frightened, realizing they must get home. The Town Hall clock struck the third hour of morning. 'Stay close to me,' he urged, but as they pushed their way through the crowd its wave-like movement seized and separated them, so the Devil was driven forward and Primo back.

Inside Maginty's, Cloete pushed his way through the club crowd to follow the stranger. He had to apprehend him, find out who he was, photograph him, make a plaster cast of his face, record the finesse of his features, document their lines and balance.

Throughout the evening, though Cloete did not know it, the Hunchback of Notre Dame – the second masked hunchback at the party – had been following him, observing his every move, watching him cavort with Snow White (her identity revealed by the clusters of rings on her fingers and her many silver bracelets). Now the figure stepped out from a corner and barred his way, leaned into him, pulled a pistol from a pocket and fired a single shot into his heart. The Hunchback of Notre Dame then spun round to face Sissy and fired twice, shattering her breastbone and pulping her lungs.

The Hunchback dropped the weapon, stepped backwards out of the door and merged into the street crowd as the club patrons, galvanized into action by the three shots, stampeded outside, screaming, 'Murderer! Hunchback! Hunchback!'

The poker players pulled off their masks and put down their cards. The club had emptied except for them, the barman and the two bodies lying in their own blood on the floor.

Dr Baldinger checked Sissy and Cloete for a pulse but found none. 'They're both dead,' he said softly. Then he called out to the barman, 'Cover them with something! And turn off the music! The party's over!'

In their apartment above Da Pasquale, Beatrice shook Pasquale awake. 'Something's happened, Pasqui! There's shooting. Someone's been shot!' A shiver of terror ran through her as she thought of Primo.

'It's nothing,' Pasquale reassured her, understanding her concern. 'Primo wasn't at the party. We would have seen him. Have you forgotten how he hates parties? It's just a gangster shooting.' He held out a hand. 'Come to bed. Come warm me. I feel so cold, so deathly cold. I am overcome by remorse for my greed of you. I have done such wrong to Primo.'

eduro had been waiting outside for Sissy. In place of a mask he wore black-lensed glasses. Sissy had dressed him in a sleeveless silver vest and tight leather trousers. His arms were oiled and they shone. She had given him a gift

225

that evening, a small articulated silver fish with emerald eyes, and this now hung from his pierced ear. The slightest movement of his head caused the fish to move – it seemed to be swimming below his lobe.

He had been leaning against Maginty's door when the first shot rang out. He turned to see the hunched figure fire into Sissy's breast, then slide out and into the mass. As Sissy crumpled to the ground and the screams of shocked revellers shredded the air, Meduro lunged into the crowd, bounding through it with little hindrance until he reached a hunchback, one no longer wearing its mask, one with a beautiful face and mahogany curls that tumbled onto his shoulders.

Meduro caught the figure from behind, shoved him through the horde of people and into Orphan Lane, where he threw him to the ground. Then he pulled from its sheath a knife, which he plunged and plunged and plunged into the breast of the black-suited figure, howling, '*Tu a tué ma Sissy! Tu a tué ma Sissy! Meurs toi aussi! Assassin!*'

Leaving the stranger for dead, he edged his way back to Maginty's where he pulled away the table-cloths that now covered the bodies, pushed Dr Baldinger aside when he tried to intervene, picked up the pistol and lifted Sissy's lifeless form. He carried her home and placed her tenderly on her bed. There he lay with her, on the white damask cover, folding his body around hers, in the sticky wet scarlet of her congealed blood, crying, with Esquire purring at their side.

Outside, sirens cut the air. Floodlights were switched on, shocking the semi-darkness. The crowd hushed as police cordoned off the area and tried to establish order.

Meanwhile the Hunchback of Notre Dame had slipped away and into Stairway to Paradise. Inside the lobby, the figure ripped off its mask and wig, cast them to the floor and strode up the stairs. The dwarfs, who had been waiting up for her, picked up what she had discarded, locked the front door and followed her. They had not opened the brothel that night so none of the other girls were in.

In her own bedroom now, Virginia, breathless, tore off the suit. She pulled out the drawer of Cloete's two-hundred rand notes and emptied it over the balcony. The money floated down to the street below. Then she took from her safe her grandmother's ruby necklace and put it on, poured herself a brandy and sat, naked, on the veranda, watching for the half-moon to set, fingering each of the jewels as though they were prayer beads.

The dwarfs took her costume out to the back and burnt everything, afterwards gathering up the ashes and flushing some down the toilet, releasing the rest to the southeast wind that came up the next day.

*　　*　　*

Primo, separated from the Devil and unable to release himself from the hold of the crowd, felt suffocated by his panic. He screamed, called out to the mass of people to yield a path so he could reach his friend. His pleas rose as vapour, unheeded. Then, as suddenly as it had tightened around him, the throng released its grip and he found himself stumbling up Orphan Lane, reaching the Devil where he lay – apparently without life – seeming to bleed from terrible wounds to the chest. With a sense of horror choking at his throat, Primo presumed the worst – that the injuries, severe enough to kill a mortal, had trapped his friend's angelic force.

Primo tore at the suit, thinking that the clothes too were a confinement, and that they were ensnaring the Devil's angelic energy. He pulled off the coat, then the dress shirt – carmine with blood – the trousers, the undergarments, the socks, the shoes, until he had just the naked winged body of an angel in his arms, its hair matted in dirt and blood, its face pale blue.

The crowd was inward-looking now, its collective mind blurred by drugs and alcohol and the rush of violence that had rippled through it. No one noticed Primo lift the Devil across his shoulder and carry him home; no one saw the great wings of the creature he carried fall forward like the useless vans of a dead albatross. If anyone had, they would have merely rubbed their alcohol-hazed eyes in disbelief.

Primo staggered under the weight of his sacred load, leant up against a traffic light to catch his breath, then stumbled home and up the steps of his stoep. He locked the door and bolted it.

Primo laid the Devil's body on his bed. He dusted off with his hands the gravel and bits of tar that clung to the wings. With warm water he sponged clean the wounds and blood; he brushed the curls. Then, with gentle care, he dressed the Devil, guiding the great wings through the openings of his robe, marvelling at the Devil's light weight now, when he had been so heavy before, amazed as the puncture wounds disappeared.

The Devil, now in his own garment – the one of rust-red silk, embroidered simply with rows of bullion knots – shuddered and opened his eyes: those deep and wondrous eyes, all-knowing like the very wells of life itself and which Primo had grown so to love.

Primo knelt at the side of the bed. 'Lucifer! I thought they had killed you,' he cried.

Outside, the dawn moved up Kloof Street, lightening up the morning.

Virginia waited for the police to track her down, but they never did. It was Meduro they arrested for double murder, finding him still curled around Sissy's bloodied body, clutching the pistol, crying while Esquire paced and meowed.

It took five men to seize him and handcuff his

arms behind his back. He fought like a wild beast being taken into captivity, knowing he would die behind bars, sensing that his captors, like the uniformed men who had stormed his village near Kinshasa and hacked his family to pieces, knew nothing of mercy and justice.

'*Maman! Ma Sissy!*' he screamed as those arresting him tore Sissy's body from his arms, kicking Esquire aside, smashing glass and sending furniture flying as they battled to harness Meduro's terrifying energy. In the struggle, they ripped his silver vest from his body and tore the fish from his ear lobe. Crimson blood dropped against his panther skin.

Virginia shut herself in her room and left the dwarfs to deal with her other prostitutes and with concerned friends and patrons. The dwarfs scurried around, frantic and wide-eyed, like two meercats whose burrows had been scorched by veld fire. Pasquale sent her a tray of food, but she ate nothing. He phoned her, but she lambasted him and told him to leave her alone. She sat on the balcony looking out at Signal Hill, drinking, thinking her own thoughts and reading, over and over again, the storybook she and Pasquale had found among their father's possessions after their parents died. It was a hand-bound book of fables written in elegant, cursive script, the faded ink speaking of a time when people wrote with fountain pens.

The author of the stories, Primus Corgatelli, was the youngest brother of the tailor, Attilio Corgatelli, who had hidden their father during the war. Their father had come to own the manuscript because, when the tailor died, the nuns who had looked after him in his senile years had posted it to Massimo. They could trace no other living relative.

Primus Corgatelli had been a journalist who wrote for the resistance newspaper *L'Italia Libera* during the years leading up to the German occupation. Following an anonymous lead he had gone to the synagogue, which also housed the Jewish community's offices, to witness and report on German soldiers confiscating the contents of Rome's Jewish library, and loading them into two railway cars marked *München*.

He knew that the library contained priceless manuscripts, incunabula, prints and books, many of which had been brought to Rome by Jews expelled from Spain and Sicily in the fifteenth century. Watching from across the road, he noted how the precious cargo was loaded into the cars, how scrolls fell to the ground and were kicked aside without respect. He should simply have made a mental note and walked on briskly without drawing attention to himself, so that he could file copy and notify his readers of this desecration. But he was also an author, a writer of tales and fantasies, a master of literature, a student of the written word. He could not stand back without protest or watch without objection as the ancient texts were transported into oblivion.

Forgetting caution, Primus strode over to the soldiers and called for an explanation.

They were angered at his effrontery. 'Are you a Jew? Or are you a lover of Jews?' one demanded, knocking him down and kicking him. 'Are you a Jew-lover?'

But the soldiers did not wait for an answer. He was arrested for hindering them in their work, detained and a week later transported with Jews to Auschwitz. Primus Corgatelli took no suitcase with him on his final journey, no identity document, no money. He had with him only what he wore: a fawn suit, tailor-made for him by his brother.

The five-day train journey had weakened him considerably. A young woman, debilitated by lack of food and water and by the foulness of the wagon, had fallen against him. He had held her up as she lapsed in and out of consciousness, whispering stories to keep her alert, knowing that if she fell down she would die.

When the transport train disgorged its cargo, he was not one who passed favourably through the first selection. His ankles were swollen, his back sprained and painful. He could barely walk. So he was not chosen to survive and work. He was selected for immediate extermination.

His suit did not go with him to the gas chamber, nor to the inferno of the crematorium. It was sent to Germany, for civilian use, with the bales of other stolen clothing. He went to his death naked, not yet fifty years of age, reciting to himself the first lines of Dante's epic: 'In the midway of this my mortal life, I found myself in a gloomy wood, astray, and gone from the direct path . . .'

It was midnight of the day after the masked party. Primo and the Devil lay together on the bed, where they had lain all day, the Devil on Beatrice's side. They listened to the melodic sounds of varied chiming as the clocks struck the hour. A single candle gave a glow to the room and picked up the glitter on the petals of a vase of paper flowers. The screech of an ambulance tore its way through the hum of Kloof Street traffic. As silence fell again, Primo heard Beatrice unlock the front door and try to open it. The bolt held it fast. She called his name.

The Devil lay still, on his back, his arms folded behind his head, his wings tucked beneath him like the hull of a barque. Both he and Primo looked up at the pressed-metal ceiling, taking pleasure in the repetitive patterns that decorated it, saying nothing, listening to Beatrice calling and to her continued knocking. Anyone able to observe the angel and the man may have noted how alike they looked, like brothers lying there; both wore embroidered robes, their hair loose and spread against the pillows.

'I'm sorry', whispered Primo, 'to have put you into such peril, to have brought you so close, so close to . . .' He could not say what he wanted to.

The Devil did not respond.

'I suppose you'll want to leave now. I'll understand that. I won't try to stop you. Only, I would ask whether I could come with you. There will be nothing for me here, once you leave. I can help you in your work. You need not be alone with the fire.'

The Devil ignored Primo's request. Instead he said, 'Shall I tell you a story?' (This is how Primo's aunt always began her tales.) 'It is the story I feel you have always wanted to know – that about God. A story which is both sad and glorious.'

'Yes,' said Primo. 'Tell me. Then perhaps I'll understand why you have been tasked as you have.'

'The story cannot be held by mere words. I would have to show you. You would have to follow me.'

'I will follow,' whispered Primo, rolling to his side so he lay against the edge of a rose-crimson wing.

The Devil spoke again and Primo felt himself tumbling, as he had tumbled into his aunt's stories, into a tale so webbed by silks of narrative and enchantment that everything material in the bedroom seemed diminished in size.

Around Primo flickered the knights and pathfinders, the light-bearers, kings and queens and humble folk who had once championed good and justice in his aunt's stories. The Devil's voice led him past these figures, beyond the plateau of the legends his aunt had known. It led him far beyond the sounds of his father's clocks so their ticking and tocking fell away like shattering crystal, taking with them time as he had always known it, and its confines. The Devil's voice, enchanting and alluring, like symphonic sound moving through layers of light, ahead of Primo, urged him not to fall behind.

Primo had the sense of a membrane tearing and yielding passage to him, allowing him entrance past great walls of galaxies, through the corridors between them where star fields hummed and pulsed. On the tips of galactic spirals, child stars exploded to life; ancient red stars burst and died, showering magma-red across interstellar black velvet. Primo became aware of an extraordinary energy, one that seemed to enter into him and align with his very heartbeat. His whole being throbbed with it.

He found himself on a great weaving, a work fashioned from pulsing energies and elaborate sequences of light. Successions of time threaded through and into each other, sequined with suns, patterned with luminosities, stitched through with the elements of silver and gold. Colours pure and rich blended with one another: scarlets; green of copper; greens of sap; browns of lichen; *sanguinaria*; safranine; white opal. Primo recognized the energies forming and re-forming in the warp and weft. They were the energies of forests and oceans, great savannahs and tundra. He was looking at the carpet of the earth but he was not on the earth. He was somewhere else. The Devil had said he was showing him God, but this was not God. This was a carpet, a matting, a weaving. He spun round, panicking, suddenly aware of his minuscule size, his inconsequence in relation to this vast, seemingly nonending masterpiece of design upon which he stood. He was but a small creature standing on a piece of woven infinity, and all about him now sounded a chorusing, a trumpeting of bird calls, the braying of wild beasts, and the sighs of fishes. He fell to his knees and saw that, embroidered into the weaving, were tiny beads. Each was a piece of life, a whale, a fish, a serpent, a bird, a mantis, a wasp, a cedar, a yellowwood, a wildebeest . . .

He became aware of deep silence falling. A wind blew, lifting the edges of the weaving and sending a ripple across it. Primo now saw that it was unravelling, that whole pieces had burned away, were charred, frayed, shredded. The threads holding the beads had been torn, so the beads were loose, scattered about, falling off the tapestry. Falling to where? he wondered. Where? Primo scrambled to gather them up, but as he touched each one it turned to sand. He leapt to his feet, sweat running down his face, terror seizing him. 'Lucifer!' he screamed and his voice echoed back from the chasms of time. 'Lucifer! Lucifer! Lucifer!'

'I am here,' said the quiet voice of the Devil, at his side. He was holding threads of light and threads of darkness, a thimble and needles of silver and gold, a handful of the tiny beads which he put into a pouch.

'There is nothing to fear, except that you will have knowledge now, when before you had none.

'Here is God's story before you – the warp and weft of creation; it is the very stitchery, composition and threading of life within life itself, for God is the true embroiderer. I only embroider celestial garments.

'This you stand upon is the mere edge of God's work, the outer side. This is the piece given to the human soul, but the human soul disrespects it. As you see, the human soul spoils it, tears it, disregards its sanctity. Look how ruined are the fibres. See how the stitching is plucked out, how the beading is picked off, how the beauty is blighted.'

'What are you showing me?' cried Primo. 'That God is nothing but a piece of carpet? That God is vulnerable? That God can be torn up by us, like a mere length of linen?'

'No,' replied the Devil, 'and yes. The two together. No – God is not vulnerable. But yes, God is. This I show you is the tearing up of the Divine masterpiece. For God is both the embroiderer and the embroidery itself. This you see is the undoing of creation – creation as the human soul knows it. This is the tapestry of the earth, nothing more, nothing less. I try to repair it. I try with my threads to restore the edges, manipulate it, rejuvenate it, restore its pristine beauty. But I am assigned much to do, as you know. And the forces of human fire and plunder are great indeed – human warring is not restricted to men alone. Mankind wars against the earth, against other species and kinds; it wars against creation itself, and therefore against the Creator. Indeed, we may speak of human evil being the greater of the powers. What strength has good in the face of this enmity?

'Now follow me, and lose not sight of me,' he urged. 'I will show you more of what you want to see, though it is not your time. Hold steady and do not be afraid. I am with you.'

Primo followed in the Devil's wake, drawn as though by white wind rushing through a tunnel of gold.

Suddenly, four archangels stepped forward, with blazing swords held high and mighty wings outstretched, diverting the Devil's passage and halting Primo. The light of the fiery angels burned Primo's eyes and he raised his hands to shield himself from their bright whiteness. His limbs grew feeble, weighing him down. He felt all his strength and movement draining from him, as though a net had been thrown over him or a powdered opiate blown into his face. His robe dissolved, like rice paper on the tongue.

He tried to hold on to the Devil's transport; he tried to grasp the Devil's energy, to realign himself with the Devil's tale. But he could not.

The archangels moved towards him.

'Who is it who dares to witness?' asked one.

'Who among us opens the door to the Afterlife,

and who among us affords a passage to this mortal?' questioned the second.

'Cast the mortal back! Or we must blind him!' said the third, striking the air with his flaming sword.

'Throw the mortal down from here! Madden him with the vision he has presumed is for other than angels,' called the fourth.

White light sliced across Primo's brow, knocking him unconscious and back through the edges of the unravelling great work, through the undoing of silk, through torn gossamers and tarnished once-lustrous weaves, through millions of tiny beads falling all about him as glitter and rain and dust storm. A black void enveloped him for endless time until he finally awoke on his bed, crying, naked, cold and shivering, drenched in sweat, feeling as though he had been thrown up from a boat wreck and cast onto a beach of stones.

The Devil was gone.

There remained where he had lain a single rose-crimson feather, powdered lightly with gold dust.

Beatrice was still banging at the door, calling Primo. He rose, painfully, to let her in.

It was five minutes past the hour of midnight.

THE END

Bibliography

David, Elizabeth. *Italian Food*. MacDonald for The Cookery Book Club. 1965, London

Jagger, Cedric. *The World's Great Clocks and Watches*. Hamlyn. 1977, London

Levi, Primo. *If this is a Man: The Truce*. Abacus. 2001, London

Piras, Claudia, and Medagliani, Eugenio (editors-in-chief). *Culinaria Italy: Pasta Pesto Passion*. Könemann Velagsgesellschaft mbH. 2000, Cologne

Sani, Gabriele. *History of the Italians in South Africa 1489–1989*. Zonderwater Block. 1992, Johannesburg

Zuccotti, Susan. *The Italians and the Holocaust: Persecution, Rescue, Survival*. Basic Books Inc. 1987, New York

Art references

Botero, Fernando (1932–   )

Colombiana che mangia una mela; *Donna che si sveste*

Buonarroti, Michelangelo (1475–1564)   *Testa di Adamo*

Burne-Jones, Sir Edward (1833–1898)   *The Beguiling of Merlin*

da Vinci, Leonardo (1452–1519)   *Testa di fanciulla*

Piero della Francesca (c. 1420-1492)   *The Resurrection*

de Morgan, Evelyn (1855–1919)   *Aurora Triumphans*

Prinsep, Valentine Cameron (1838–1904)   *Leonora de Mantua*

Rossetti, Dante Gabriel (1828–1882)

Girl at a Lattice; *Beata Beatrix*; *Bocca Baciata*

Artist unknown – dated 1952   *The Doge's Palace*

Italian prisoners of war (1940s)   A mural depicting Saint Francis in Italian fields, and the Virgin Mary in an arcaded Tuscan courtyard. (Chapel of St Francis, known as 'The Italian Chapel', five kilometres east of Masvingo, on the main Mutare road, Zimbabwe.)

Glossary

Agnello alla pastora (It.) Lamb and potato casserole cooked with tomato and pecorino cheese

Amaretto (It.) A macaroon

Anisetta (It.) A liqueur made from star aniseed and other aromatic ingredients

Basilico (It.) Sweet basil

Beata Beatrix (Lat.) Blessed Beatrice

Bergie (Afrik.) Vagrant; homeless person

Biscotti (It.) Biscuits

Boerebeskuit (Afrik.) Rusk

Boerewors Traditional South African sausage

Bostrengo (It.) A rich sweet rice cake traditional to Marche, near Umbria

Brioche (It.) A small rounded sweet roll made with a light yeast dough

Budino Toscano (It.) A dessert made with ricotta, ground almonds and candied orange peel

Bunnychows   Vegetarian curry sold as a take-away in a hollowed-out half-loaf of bread

'Calmati! Sta calma! Ti prego!' (It.)   'Calm down! I beg you!'

Camomilla (It.)   Camomile

Canneloni (It.)   Tubes of pasta generally filled with meat or cheese

Carciofi alla Veneziana (It.)   Stewed artichokes

Challah (Heb.)   Shabbat bread – plaited for Shabbat and rounded for Rosh Hashana

Chiaroscuro (It.)   The treatment of light and shade in painting and drawing

Cotechino (It.)   Pork sausage

Credenza (pl. credenze) (It.)   Sideboard

Il Duce (It.)   Benito Mussolini. Italian dictator, founder and leader of the Italian Fascist party

Festa del Sacro Cuore (It.)   Feast day of the Sacred Heart

Filone (It.)   Classic Tuscan unsalted bread

Focaccia (It.)   Flat unleavened bread

Fontina (It.)   A creamy Piedmontese cheese

Frittatine di patate e zafferano (It.)   Potato cakes with saffron

Fynbos (Afrik.)   Narrow-leaved evergreen shrubs indigenous to the Western Cape

Grappa (It.)   A clear spirit distilled from the remains of grapes after pressing

L'Inferno (It.)   Hell; title of first part of Dante's *Divine Comedy*

Koeksisters (Afrik.)   A deep-fried twisted sweet doughnut

Kwerekwere (Xhosa or Zulu) Foreigner; generally from Africa, and living in South Africa illegally

Langarm (Afrik.) 'Pump-handle' style of dancing with both partners' arms extended

Lasagna verde (It.) Green lasagne

Lekker (Afrik.) Nice; pleasant. A term of general approbation

Mampoer (Afrik.) Home-distilled spirit made from soft fruits

Mbira (Shona) Musical instrument played with the thumbs, either over or inside a calabash

Miele e ricotta (It.) Dessert made with ricotta cheese and honey

Ménage à trois (French) A threesome; domestic triangle

Moffie (Afrik. slang) Homosexual or transvestite

Muti (Zulu) Spells, herbs, animal and human body parts used in traditional therapy, witchcraft or magic

N'anga (Shona) A diviner; a healer with supernatural powers

Orto (It.) Kitchen garden

Ossobuco (It.) Stewed knuckle of veal

Palazzo (It.) Palace

Panettone (It.) Spiced cake

Panforte Senese (It.) Dessert made with nuts and candied fruits

Pantalone (It.) The Simpleton; **Pulcinella** (It.) The Old Merchant: Venetian masks and costumes

Parmigiana di melanzane alla Calabrese (It.) Aubergines baked with minced beef, Parmesan and herbs

Pecorino (It.)   Sheep's milk cheese

Peperoni (It.)   Peppers

Polenta alla Madiba (It.)   Polenta (maize meal) cooked Madiba-style

Polenta pasticciata (It.)   Polenta (maize meal) pie

Polpetta (It.)   Rissole of meat with herbs

Poste restante (Fr.)   Post held for collection when delivery is not possible

Provolone (It.)   A soft but firm-textured pale yellow cheese

Ragù (It.)   Meat sauce

Regina Mundi (Lat.)   Queen of the World

Sacra Vergine (It.)   Sacred Virgin

Salomies (Afrik.)   Round flat bread spread with curry stuffing and rolled up

Salsa pizzaiola (It.)   Sauce richly flavoured with garlic and herbs

Sangoma (Xhosa)   A diviner; a healer with supernatural powers

Santa Maria (It.)   Holy Mary

Schiacciatina (It.)   A small flat salted bread

Skottel braais (Afrik.)   Wok-type griddle for use on fire or gas-burner

Slap (Afrik.)   Limp; but in this case referring to fried potato chips

Sosaties (Afrik.)   Cubes of curried meat on a skewer

Sotto olio (It.)   (Served) in oil

Stoep (Afrik.)   Verandah

Strega (It.)   A herbal liqueur

Swart gevaar (Afrik.)   Black peril

Tambotie A rare protected South African free with highly aromatic wood, which releases toxic smoke when burnt

Tiramisu (It.) Dessert made from mascarpone cheese and boudoir biscuits

Torta nera (It.) A tart of almonds, coffee, cocoa, lemon and liqueur

Tortellini alla Romagnola (It.) Tortellini filled with turkey

'Tu a tué ma Sissy! Meurs toi aussi! Assassin!' (Fr.) 'You have killed my Sissy! Die yourself as well! Murderer!'

Vaporetto (It.) Venetian boat-taxi

Vetkoek (Afrik.) A savoury deep-fried cake made of yeasted dough, similar to a doughnut

Vitello alla Genovese (It.) Veal cooked with white wine and artichokes

Zabaglione (It.) Dessert made with egg yolk and Marsala

Zia Lidia (It.) Aunt Lidia

THE APOTHECARY'S DAUGHTER

Patricia Schonstein

A nobleman and his wife, an apothecary nun, an astronomer-mathematician, an inquisitor, a poet who is both lover and villain, a portraitist, a queen and loyal servants deftly act out a beautiful drama of tantalizing relationships.

They take up their roles in castle and convent, some surrounded by ornate interiors, garbed in velvets and silks, garlanded with precious jewels; while others abide in simple space devoid of art or representation, and dressed in plain linens and dull calicos.

The Apothecary's Daughter is a wondrous tale, rendered in erotic prose and poetry, stitched through with rich imagery, humour and tenderness. It is also a story of trade and exotic travel, both across the surface of the earth and among the stars.

0 593 05178 5

NOW AVAILABLE FROM BANTAM PRESS

PEOPLE LIKE OURSELVES

Pamela Jooste

'HER WRITING IS CLEAR, LIGHT AND SHARPLY OBSERVANT'
Barbara Trapido, *Spectator*

Julia belongs to the inner circle of Johannesburg high society. But in the New South Africa, things have changed – the days of tea on the lawn are over.

Julia's husband, Douglas, is a serial adulterer who is no longer prepared to pay for the small luxuries she has always enjoyed. Her daughter has rebelled herself right out of Julia's life. She doesn't seem to be able to manage the 'home workers' who seem to have developed a will of their own, and her best friend, Caroline, is quietly considering killing her husband.

Now Douglas's ex-wife, who is never spoken of, has announced her intention of coming to visit from London bringing, no doubt, her politically correct credentials along with her. She's coming to see Nelson Mandela, she says.

People Like Ourselves takes a wry look at the brave new world that is the 'African miracle' today, by the prize-winning author of *Frieda and Min*, *Like Water in Wild Places* and *Dance with a Poor Man's Daughter*.

'PERCEPTIVE AND SENSITIVE AND EXTREMELY FUNNY'
The Times

'JOOSTE IS A SIGNIFICANT VOICE IN SOUTH AFRICAN WRITING . . . SHE CHALLENGES US TO SEE THE HURT, THE ANXIETY, THE TRUTHS'
Cape Argus

'FEW NOVELISTS HAVE WRITTEN ABOUT THE NEW SOUTH AFRICA IN THIS ACCESSIBLE, HUMOROUS AND INSIGHTFUL WAY, TO REVEAL A DARING AND PROVOCATIVE VISION OF LIFE AFTER TRUTH AND RECONCILIATION'
The Cape Times

0 552 99871 0

BLACK SWAN

FIVE QUARTERS OF THE ORANGE

Joanne Harris

Beyond the main street of Les Laveuses runs the Loire, smooth and brown as a sunning snake – but hiding a deadly undertow beneath its moving surface. This is where Framboise, a secretive widow named after a raspberry liqueur, plies her culinary trade at the crêperie – and lets her memory play strange games.

Into this world comes the threat of revelation as Framboise's nephew – a profiteering Parisian – attempts to exploit the growing success of the country recipes she has inherited from her mother, a woman remembered with contempt by the villagers of Les Laveuses. As the spilt blood of a tragic wartime childhood flows again, exposure beckons for Framboise, the widow with an invented past.

0 552 99883 4

BLACK SWAN

A SELECTED LIST OF FINE WRITING
AVAILABLE FROM BLACK SWAN

77115 5	**BRICK LANE**	*Monica Ali*	£7.99
99588 6	**THE HOUSE OF THE SPIRITS**	*Isabel Allende*	£7.99
77105 8	**NOT THE END OF THE WORLD**	*Kate Atkinson*	£6.99
99863 X	**MARLENE DIETRICH LIVED HERE**	*Eleanor Bailey*	£6.99
77121 X	**THE HOTTEST DAY OF THE YEAR**	*Brinda Charry*	£6.99
99767 6	**SISTER OF MY HEART**	*Chitra Banerjee Divakaruni*	£6.99
99836 2	**A HEART OF STONE**	*Renate Dorrestein*	£6.99
99935 0	**PEACE LIKE A RIVER**	*Leif Enger*	£6.99
99954 7	**SWIFT AS DESIRE**	*Laura Esquivel*	£6.99
77182 1	**THE TIGER BY THE RIVER**	*Ravi Shankar Etteth*	£6.99
99721 8	**BEFORE WOMEN HAD WINGS**	*Connie May Fowler*	£6.99
99978 4	**KISSING THE VIRGIN'S MOUTH**	*Donna Gershten*	£6.99
99656 4	**THE TEN O'CLOCK HORSES**	*Laurie Graham*	£5.99
99890 7	**DISOBEDIENCE**	*Jane Hamilton*	£6.99
99883 4	**FIVE QUARTERS OF THE ORANGE**	*Joanne Harris*	£6.99
77005 1	**IN THE KINGDOM OF MISTS**	*Jane Jakeman*	£6.99
99871 0	**PEOPLE LIKE OURSELVES**	*Pamela Jooste*	£6.99
99996 2	**EVA'S COUSIN**	*Sibylle Knauss*	£6.99
77106 6	**LITTLE INDISCRETIONS**	*Carmen Posadas*	£6.99
99909 1	**LA CUCINA**	*Lily Prior*	£6.99
77087 6	**GIRL FROM THE SOUTH**	*Joanna Trollope*	£6.99
99864 8	**A DESERT IN BOHEMIA**	*Jill Paton Walsh*	£6.99
99673 4	**DINA'S BOOK**	*Herbjørg Wassmo*	£7.99
99723 4	**PART OF THE FURNITURE**	*Mary Wesley*	£6.99
77107 4	**SPELLING MISSISSIPPI**	*Marnie Woodrow*	£6.99
77101 5	**PAINTING RUBY TUESDAY**	*Jane Yardley*	£6.99